LADY KNIGHT

Crystal Journals 3

G. Rosemary Ludlow

This is a work of fiction. All o f the characters, organizations and events portrayed in this novel are either the products of the author's imagination or are used fictitiously.

Summary: Young time traveler, Susan Sinclair, and her cousin are transported to medieval Europe in 1212 to help a royal run-away save the future emperor, Frederick, from those plotting against him.

© 2017 G. Rosemary Ludlow

Cover Design: Diogo Lando

Library and Archives Canada Cataloguing in Publication

ISBN: 0973687150
EAN: 9780973687156
EBook: ISBN: 9780973687163

1. Europe 2. Time Travel 3. Fantasy and Magic 4. Friendship 5. Preteen

Published by: Comwave Publishing House Inc.,
Vancouver, BC, Canada

For All Children everywhere
Young and Old

I create these stories for your enjoyment.

THE STORY SO FAR

Book 1, A Rare Gift, tells the story of how Susan Sinclair receives a crystal at a flea market. A lady gives it to her, but it is more correct to say that the crystal chose Susan. Unfortunately Susan doesn't wait to hear what is important about the crystal but wanders off into the crowd.

She wakes up on a sailing ship in the middle of the Atlantic Ocean. Susan has no idea where she is or how she got there, but she does know that she doesn't like it. And she doesn't like the boy, Jeremy, who sneers at her and accuses her of trying to steal his knife.

In a later meeting with the lady, Mrs. Coleman, Susan learns that there are four crystals and she is now the Guardian of the Crystal of the North and that it will lead her to places where there is an imbalance or unfairness in the world and that she will be able to help correct the situation.

Susan gradually grows into her role and Jeremy and Susan have many adventures and help many children before the first story is fully told. Mrs. Coleman gives Susan an envelope containing instructions for how to use the crystal. She gifts Susan with the bag she used during her travels.

◄═╋ ╋═►

In Book 2, Pharaoh's Tomb, Susan is pulled away very suddenly. As she travels back through time her crystal fades from her hand. She arrives in Ancient Egypt with no crystal to take her back to her family.

A magician has pulled her to him. He needs her help to create the crystals. She is in a time before her crystal was formed. Her only way home is to work with this ambitious and self-centered man to create the crystals. In the six months it takes the crystals to form Susan lives as a princess within the court of the pharaoh, Tuthmoses II. She makes friends and foes as she learns to live in this totally different culture.

By the time her crystal is fully formed and calling to her, tragedy has removed it from her reach. She must show courage and resolution to retrieve her crystal and bid her new friends goodbye.

She arrives home just ahead of an Australian cousin, Jason, who is resting between bouts of treatment for cancer.

And now to Book 3, Lady Knight.

CHAPTER 1
IT BEGINS

Susan and Jason sat together at a small table. Susan riffled through the jigsaw pieces until she found another border piece.

"Here," she said, handing the piece to Jason.

"Thanks," he said, taking it from her.

Susan looked for another piece.

Sunshine streamed through the window and fell across a corner of their table.

Susan could see the garden from where she sat. Their parents were gathered around the picnic table, chatting. Jason's dad had his feet up on a stump. As Susan watched, somebody said something, and the laughter of all four rolled up the side of the house and in the open window.

The shady maple tree by the garden swing looked so inviting. But Jason felt weak right now. Most days he was able to go outside and sit in the garden, but not today.

Susan wore a T-shirt and jeans; Jason was rugged up in a shirt and a sweater and had a throw rug over his knees. Occasionally Susan saw that he would shiver a little, even though he tried to make it so she didn't notice.

Susan found a corner piece. "Here, this will help." She handed the piece to Jason.

"Hey, thanks," he said, taking the piece from her and positioning it. Then he looked up and smiled at her. "Not much fun being stuck inside on such a lovely day, is it?" He shuffled a couple of pieces around with his fingers. "I know," he said. "I've spent way too many days inside, looking out the window." He looked up at Susan again. "I will beat this cancer, I truly will, but in the meantime, I just have to be patient and do what I can." Jason shrugged. "Today that's a jigsaw puzzle." He shook his head. "But not for you. Go visit Judy. You can help me finish up the picture when you get back."

It was Susan's turn to shake her head. "It's OK, Jason, really. I think you're beyond brave, and I like your company. I'm just used to being outside a lot more, that's all."

"Go then." Jason flapped his hands at her.

"I'll stay." Susan turned her attention back to the puzzle. A picture of a sailing ship was emerging on the table. *Of all the subjects to pick*, Susan thought. *At least it's a clipper ship and not one full of immigrants.* Susan gave a shiver of her own at the memory.

Then another shiver. Her crystal tingled on her thigh. It was in the pocket of her jeans. *Oh no!* Susan stood up so quickly that her chair tipped over behind her. "I...I have to go to my room for a while, Jason. I...I won't be long." Susan rushed across the family room and slammed the door of her bedroom behind her.

A crystal journey now! With Jason in the next room! She bustled around. Susan grabbed her bag with the things she would need. She wrapped a long skirt on over her pants and grabbed the woolen coat that hung behind the door—just as the door opened. Susan jumped back. Jason stood in the doorway.

"Susan, I don't want you to be angry." Jason took a step into the room. His expression changed from worry to astonishment. "Susan, you're fading." He rushed toward her.

"It's all right, Jason. Don't worry. It happens to me sometimes." Susan tried to smile. Her world was slipping, sliding. "I'll be back soon."

"Don't fade." Jason grabbed her arm. "I've got you."

Susan world totally slipped. She shook her arm to make Jason let go. *I have some explaining to do when I get back.* The sliding colors slid; the noises blended into one sound. *Here I go again.* Susan hoped she wouldn't land in mud this time.

"Oof." Susan landed on soft green grass. Sheep grazed nearby, and a couple of lambs romped about.

"Ouch." Jason rubbed his head. He was sitting beside her.

CHAPTER 2
WHAT HAPPENED!

"Jason, what are you doing here?" Susan stared. "You can't be here," she said.

"Where's here?" Jason asked, still rubbing his head.

Susan shook her head. "I don't know yet."

"What do you mean you don't know?" Jason glared. "Is this a joke? Did I pass out or something?"

"It's no joke." Susan sighed. "It's my life."

"How can you not know where this is?" Jason looked around. "It looks pretty nice. I guess we're close to your house, but I can't see it."

Susan shook her head again. She reached over and touched Jason's arm. "It's usually not so much a matter of where I am as *when* I am." She scanned the area. "This looks safe enough for now," she added.

"Safe." Jason's voice was rising. "Safe," he yelled. "What do you mean safe? I have to take my next medication in an hour. We better be back home by then."

"I'll try to explain," Susan said. And she did. Susan showed him the crystal. She explained about her responsibilities to set things right in the world. She told him about Jeremy and the immigrant ship and even about her time in Egypt. She finished by saying, "I guess you traveled with me because you grabbed my arm. I should be able to take you back."

Jason leaped to his feet. "I've never heard such a load of malarkey in all my life." He stamped his foot and put his hands on his hips. "This looks like the paddocks around your place to me." He turned on his heel. "This is some sort of trick." He began striding across the grass. "I'm off," he said.

Susan stood, too. She stared, openmouthed, at her cousin stomping off across the field.

"Jason," she called. And then she yelled. "Jason!" He kept going.

Susan ran after him. She had trouble catching up. "Jason, stop a minute," she puffed.

Jason stopped on the top of a small rise. He looked around. He turned full circle, shaking his head.

Susan reached Jason there. She grabbed his arm. He glared at her.

"Look at yourself," she panted. "Just take a moment and look at yourself and where you are and what you just did."

Jason dropped to his knees. He drew a deep, deep breath, then another one. He looked up at Susan with excitement in his eyes.

"I just jumped up and stomped across a whole paddock and up a hill, and I'm not even puffing."

Susan nodded, smiling. "Yes, you did."

Jason jumped to his feet and twirled around full circle. "I feel wonderful. I can't remember the last time I felt this good." He felt his torso and ran his hands down his arms and legs. "Nothing hurts," he said in wonder.

Susan sighed with relief. "This must be an effect of the crystal." She looked at Jason closely. She walked around him as he stood tall and straight with his hands on his hips. "You're still extremely thin, but you look so healthy all of a sudden."

Jason grabbed Susan in a bear hug. "Thank you, thank you, this is so great."

Over Jason's shoulder, Susan noticed a bearded man striding up the rise toward them. He wore a long tunic and leggings with sandals on his feet and a woven straw hat on his head. He carried a shepherd's crook in one hand—and he was waving it at them.

Susan stepped away from Jason to greet the man, and Jason turned to see what had caught Susan's attention.

"Hey, you pilgrims, get away from my sheep," the shepherd yelled. "I already lost one this week. Get on your way." He kept coming toward them.

"Quick." She gasped. "We need to run, right now." She grabbed Jason's arm and dragged him back down the hill and away.

"What's happening? Why are we running?" Jason wanted to know.

"Just run," Susan insisted and kept going flat out. She spotted a dirt track along a creek and headed for that.

Bang. Something hit her squarely in the middle of her back. She turned to see the shepherd placing another stone into a strip of leather. "Quick, quick," she called to Jason. "Go as fast as you can and dodge about—he's got a slingshot."

When they reached the track, they hurried into the shelter of a stand of trees.

From the shelter of the forest, Susan watched the shepherd. First he paced, glaring at the forest, but soon his flock drew his attention, and he tucked his slingshot into his waistband and walked back up the hill.

The two slumped into the grass beside the track. "What was that all about?" Jason asked.

"He thought we were pilgrims and wanted to steal a sheep."

"How do you know that?"

Susan shrugged. "He was yelling about how he had already lost a sheep to the pilgrims."

"Yeah, he was yelling," Jason agreed, "but not in any language I know."

Susan chuckled. She remembered.

I had just arrived in Egypt. No crystal. No way home. The magician, Harsheer, in his workshop, crystal mixture bubbling. Him pulling jars and boxes off the shelves and mixing up another potion. A smell that grabbed my nose and made it hard to breathe. Then shoving half of it down my throat. Ugh. The thought makes me want to spit. But. I could understand. And when I opened my mouth I spoke Egyptian. It's still working. Susan thought.

"The crystal lets me understand what everyone is saying, and they understand me," was all she said.

Jason threw himself back onto the grass and sheltered his face with his arm. "This isn't a trick, is it?" he said. "We're really somewhere—some when different."

"Looks like it," was all Susan said.

Susan waited. She watched Jason. She could almost hear him thinking. *It takes a while to come to accept what has happened.*

Eventually he sat up and looked at her with a smile. "Well. Whatever. I feel great." He flexed his arms. "I feel strong, and best of all, I don't hurt." Then he grinned. "I'm hungry. Got any food in that bag of yours?"

With a laugh, Susan fished around to see what she had. She pulled out some trail mix tied up in a cloth. "Here, this will tide you over until we can find something else."

Jason grabbed a handful. "Why tie it up in a cloth? Why not use a plastic bag?"

Susan shrugged. "It's a good idea to try to blend in. I never know what to expect. The first time I arrived in jeans and everyone thought I was a boy."

Jason snorted as he chewed. "With your hair that short, they'll still think you're a boy—even wearing that skirt."

"True." Susan set the bag on her lap and rummaged around until she found a scarf. She tied it around her head.

"Better." Jason nodded.

He jumped to his feet, and swinging his arms, he took in a big, deep breath. He blew it out and took another. "I feel great!" he said. And jumped high into the air. He landed. Looked down at his feet and laughed.

"What's so funny?" Susan wanted to know.

Jason plopped down beside her again. "I've just realized how lucky it is that I decided to get dressed and to put on my runners this morning. I could be standing here in my pajamas and slippers." He waved his hand at Susan's bag. "I bet there's not a change of clothes for me in there."

Susan laughed, too. She looked at this joyful, happy boy, so full of life all of a sudden, and she thought back to the pale and wispy boy he had been that morning, slowly working on a jigsaw puzzle.

An idea struck.

"Jason, maybe you're why we're here. Maybe the crystal dragged us here as a way to heal you because you were so sick."

Jason swept an imaginary hat from his head and executed a deep bow. "Thank you, crystal," he said.

"Well, we should be able to go back now."

"No way. I want to explore. This is the most interesting thing to happen to me since I was stranded in the bush as a toddler. And I hardly remember that."

Chattering voices intruded on their conversation. They kept quiet to listen. The voices drew closer.

Susan put her finger to her lips. Jason nodded, and they both slipped among the trees and lay down where they hoped they wouldn't be seen.

CHAPTER 3
THE CHILDREN

From their hiding place, Susan and Jason listened as the high-pitched chatter drew closer. *It sounds like a bunch of children*, Susan thought.

As they watched, a straggling group of children came along the dusty track. They were of different ages. Some of the older children carried small ones. The entire group looked tired and footsore, but still, an air of excitement hung over the group. Most of the chatter centered on meeting someone called Nicholas. They were traveling together to hear someone called Nicholas speak. The children chattered about the meeting and acted as though they were on a great adventure—that they were going to change the world.

Susan shook her head. For all their brave talk and excitement, the children were bone thin, their hair was matted, and their faces dirty. Half of the children wore no shoes, and only one had a warm cloak around her shoulders.

Susan noticed this girl in particular. She wore shoes—stout leather shoes. Her dress was made of closely woven wool and, although dusty, looked to be of good quality. She moved quietly along the road with the other children, not chatting or excited. The others seemed to accept her into their group, but none of them spoke to her as they walked along. She carried a heavy bag over her shoulder and was helping a couple of the smaller children along.

Susan guessed she was about fifteen. *She looks so sad*, Susan noticed. The girl looked back over her shoulder several times as she walked along the path.

In a matter of minutes, the group had straggled past the spot where Susan and Jason hid. The two waited for a moment before standing. They needed to stretch to get the kinks out.

"What a group," Jason commented, bending down to touch his toes.

Susan nodded as she stretched her arms above her head. "There is certainly something odd going on," she said. "Why would all those children be out on the road without an adult? They looked painfully thin and not at all well dressed for traveling."

"Except that pretty one," Jason added. "She was better dressed and looked better fed. She was one of the oldest of the group, too, I think."

"Yes, she certainly was different. The others seemed to sense it, too." Susan picked up her bag. "She didn't look excited about Nicholas like the others, either. I wonder why she is with them."

"Let's follow and find out," Jason suggested with a grin. "Maybe you're supposed to help them. Maybe that's why you're here, and I just tagged along by grabbing your arm."

"Possible," Susan agreed. "We should see what's happening, I guess. Let's go."

Susan and Jason set off along the track in the wake of the children. They could hear their voices up ahead, and as they didn't want to get too close, they lagged along.

"This is pretty thick forest here." Jason peered into the forest beside the track. He looked up. "Look how tall these trees are."

Susan sniffed the air. "Smells really fresh," she said, "but not like the pine forests at home." She waved her hand at the trees. "Look how straight they are and not many branches until you get way up there in the sunlight."

Jason moved to the side of the track. "And look, there's little trees growing around the base of the bigger ones." He pointed into the forest.

Susan joined him at the side of the track. "It's certainly beautiful. So green but quite dark compared to the field where the sheep grazed."

Jason pointed up. "Look, the trees meet above us. I guess they're sucking up most of the sunlight."

Susan and Jason strolled along, content to take in their surroundings for the moment.

"I wonder what happens when it gets dark."

"Hmmph, don't expect a motel around the next corner," Susan informed him.

"Huh. What other food have you got in that bag of yours?" Jason wanted to know.

CHAPTER 4
HORSES

The two walked along the path in companionable silence. Susan dug out her trail mix, and they munched handfuls as they followed the group of children.

"Yuk, ginger." Jason screwed up his face. "What's ginger doing in here?" He opened his hand, examining the nuts and dried fruit on his palm. "There's more," he said and started picking out the little sugary pieces.

"Yum, my favorite." Susan leaned over, took out the ginger, and popped it in her mouth. "Dad always puts lots of ginger in the mix, just for me."

"You make it?" Jason peered at his palm. "What else is in here?"

Susan laughed. "It's all good stuff. That's why we make our own. Dad gets all the dried fruits and nuts, and we sit around the table and cut up some of the big pieces and mix it just how we like to have it. It's fun."

Jason shook his head. "I've nev—" He broke off. Horses. More than one. Coming up behind them. Pounding hooves. Coming fast.

"Make way. Make way," Susan heard, and three horses, at full gallop, came careering down the path behind them.

Jason and Susan leaped to safety just in time. Through the choking dust kicked up by the horses, Susan glimpsed the backs of the riders as they thundered around the curve ahead. They looked to be knights, soldiers at least. In a flash Susan saw swords, helmets, and what looked like chain mail. Then they were gone. Out of sight. But Susan and Jason could still hear the pounding hooves ahead of them.

"The children." Susan gasped, jumping to her feet. "They won't be able to get out of the way."

Jason peered ahead. "I hope they slow down."

They heard yelling and screams.

Jason jumped up and began running down the path toward the children.

Susan set off after him. "Wait," she called. But Jason didn't wait. He turned to her, running backward. "We have to help," he yelled, then turned and ran on.

Susan ran as hard as she could. Her bag banged against her thigh, but she used one hand to steady it. Finally, she reached for and caught Jason's arm. "Stop a minute," she whispered. "It's no good rushing in before we know what will be the best way to help."

Jason stopped in his tracks. "You're right," he said. "But we have to do something."

"Of course," Susan said and pulled Jason into the trees beside the road.

"Come on. Keep hidden," Susan whispered.

The two of them slipped as quietly and quickly as they could through the trees toward the spot where they could hear yelling and crying.

Through the trees, they could see the horses grazing beside the track. Then they saw the men. Each held a child by the arms. One of the knights was shaking the tallest boy of the group.

"Where is she?" the knight yelled as he rattled the boy.

"Where's who?" the boy replied. The knight shook him harder and then pulled his sword from its sheath and began waving it about.

One of the other knights came up to the pair. "Let me, Sir Gustaff," he said and pulled the boy toward him.

Sir Gustaff, still in a temper, stormed off and kicked at the tufts of grass along the road.

The other children stood around; they looked unsure of what to do. Little ones were crying, and some of the older children tried to comfort them. Sir Gustaff made a threatening movement toward them, and they squealed and fell back. More of them began to cry.

Sir Gustaff laughed at their fear.

That is not a nice laugh, Susan decided.

Susan and Jason bent low and slipped closer.

Jason touched Susan's arm and pointed to the side. There, crouching behind a fallen log, was the girl from the group. The one who looked better dressed and better fed than the others. As they watched, she sank deeper into the undergrowth so that she could barely be seen. She looked scared.

Susan turned her attention back to the group of children.

The knight who had taken the boy from Sir Gustaff settled him on his feet and began to talk to him quietly. Susan moved closer to hear what he said.

"She's about this high," the knight said, holding his arm out to about Susan's height. "She has long black hair that reaches almost to her waist." The boy looked at him from under his eyelashes. He said nothing.

"It's very important that we find her," the knight continued, looking around at all the children. They hung their heads.

"She is probably wearing a blue cloak," the third knight interjected. Several of the children looked up at this.

"Ah, huh." Sir Gustaff grunted. "I knew it. She's hiding somewhere here."

The tall boy found his voice. "We're all pilgrims. Sacred pilgrims. We're going to the holy land. God will protect us."

"You're children," snarled Sir Gustaff, and swinging his sword at the undergrowth, he plowed into the forest, searching. As he searched, Susan heard him muttering, "Found her book in the garden. Looked for her everywhere. There was her book. The little slip had been listening to us. Have to find her."

Susan looked toward the place where the girl lay hidden in the bushes. She saw a hint of the blue cloak through the leaves.

"Quick," she said to Jason. "Take my bag. Keep her hidden."

With that she crept over to the hiding place. The girl was so intent on peeping out to see what was happening on the road that she started when Susan touched her arm.

Susan raised her fingers to her lips. "Shhhh," she breathed, as she carefully and quietly slipped the girl's cloak from around her shoulders and put it on. She pulled the deep hood up so that her face was completely hidden.

Then Susan stood, braced her shoulders, and walked through the undergrowth straight into trouble.

"Oh," she squealed as soon as she reached the road. "Oh," she squealed a little louder to be sure she had attracted everyone's attention. "What's happening?" She flapped her hands, trying to look distressed and scared.

Sir Gustaff was by her side in a second. He grabbed her arm in a cruel grip and ripped the hood from her head.

"Her cloak. Not her," he exclaimed, pushing Susan into the dust. Then he leaned down and grabbed the cloak from Susan. "It's her cloak," he exclaimed, waving it in the air. "Where did you get it, wretch?"

It looked to Susan as though Sir Gustaff was getting ready to kick her. "She gave it to me, sir," she stammered. She was truly scared now. What had she got herself into?

"Where, where?" Sir Gustaff screamed.

Susan climbed painfully and slowly to her feet. *Stall as long as possible*, she thought.

"Um, um." She started to cry. Big, noisy sobs and wails. That set some of the other children off as well.

Sir Gustaff grabbed her shoulders and shook her. "Where, where?"

Still sobbing loudly, Susan pointed back down the road in the direction they had come.

"Right." Sir Gustaff bundled up the cloak and threw it across his saddle. "Come on. We must have missed her." He mounted his horse.

The gentler knight came up to his side and pulled the blue cloak away from him. He turned to Susan with it in his hands.

"Hey, Sir Robert," Sir Gustaff protested. "That's hers."

Sir Robert shook his head. "Katerina wanted this girl to have it," he said and handed the cloak to Susan.

A little boy, who had been standing beside the road, watching everything intently, then burst out. "But that's not—" He got a clout from a bigger boy, who sat beside the road with his hat pulled well over his face.

Susan took the cloak and swirled it around her shoulders to try to draw attention away from the little boy.

"They're pilgrims," Sir Robert said. "They are protected by God."

"They're children, peasant children," Sir Gustaff sneered and yanked on his reins to turn his horse back down the road.

Sir Robert grabbed the reins of his horse, but before he mounted, he opened his saddlebag. "Here," he said to Susan. He had food in his hands. "I can get more for myself." He mounted and rode after Sir Gustaff.

The third knight grabbed at his horse. "Wait, Gustaff, wait," he called. "I'm coming." And then he, too, mounted his horse and rode away.

Susan sagged to the ground beside the track. Her heart felt like it was banging in her throat.

A waterskin was thrust at her. She looked up to see the boy from the side of the road. He was offering her a drink.

"That was bravely done," he said, sitting beside her. "My name is Watt."

"Thanks for the water." Susan took a sip. "What is happening here? What was that all about?"

"It's not my story to tell." Watt shook his head.

CHAPTER 5
MEET KATERINA

Once the knights galloped off, the children gathered their bundles and began straggling down the road again. They weren't chattering now, and Susan heard a few sniffles and hiccoughs as they moved past her.

Susan stood when she heard rustling in the undergrowth. She saw Jason and the girl moving through the trees to join them. Jason had her arm nestled in the crook of his elbow as he helped her through the shrubs. She held her skirts in her free hand.

He looks like he's escorting her to the prom, Susan thought with a chuckle.

They stepped out onto the dusty track. The girl looked right and then left. She quickly spotted Susan and moved to join her.

Susan removed the blue cloak and held it out to her. "I assume you are Katerina," Susan said.

"You took my cloak." Katerina declared. "Why?"

"He was going to come looking for you, swinging that sword of his," Susan answered with a shrug.

Katerina nodded. "But he is Sir Gustaff. He is all-powerful in this area. Nobody flouts his authority."

Susan shrugged again. "Well, I did," she said and took her bag back from Jason, who stood shoulder to shoulder with her.

"Why?"

Susan thought about it for a moment. "Well," she said. "I didn't like him. He was dangerous. He was going to capture you, and I didn't want him to."

Katerina looked surprised. She picked up her bundle, which was lying beside the track and turned to Susan. She gave a quick bow of her head. "Thank you," she said and set off along the road after the other children. Watt jumped up and followed her.

Jason linked his hand in Susan's, and they set off, too. "They've got food. Come on," he said.

They walked in silence for a while, but then Jason shoulder-bumped her and said, "Susan, you really did help back there. Are you all right? You got knocked down by that thug."

Susan rolled her shoulders. "Yes, I'm fine. I wish I knew where we were and what was happening, though."

Jason laughed. "Hmm, we're somewhere—in a forest. We're going somewhere else along a dirt track. We're with a bunch of kids all ages and sizes. We've been attacked by a shepherd who thought we were stealing his sheep. And—and let's not forget—three knights who thought you were someone else. Am I right so far?" Then he patted his stomach. "And I'm still hungry."

Susan laughed, too. "Welcome to my life," she said. Then she shook her head. "I really do have to learn more history."

Jason nodded emphatically.

CHAPTER 6
BY THE CAMPFIRE

As soon as the sun sank below the trees, the children gathered in a small clearing beside the road and began to set up a camp. They lit small fires and spread their blankets on the ground.

Katerina and Watt settled on the edge of the group. They were standoffish around the other children. Susan decided to find out a little more about what was happening and dropped her bag close to Katerina's. She sat cross-legged on the grass with a sigh.

Katerina glared at her. "This is our space," she said haughtily.

"It's forest." Susan looked around. "Doesn't seem to have a name on it."

"Well, actually, it belongs to Sir Gustaff's father," Katerina said. And then she smiled.

"Uh-oh." Susan shook her head and smiled back.

It felt to Susan that the ice had broken. She relaxed, and she could see that Katerina had relaxed, too. They both stared off, idly watching the children settle on the ground.

Watt rose from his position and wandered over to where food was being distributed.

Susan counted. Twelve children were spread around the clearing. The biggest boy looked about fifteen years old, but although tall, he was thin. His hair hung past his ears. He looked tired and careworn. His clothes were patched and ragged.

"That's Grefin." Katerina leaned toward her. "He's been traveling for almost two weeks. He gathered these children as he came."

"But why?" Susan wanted to know. "Surely they are too young to be away from their homes and parents."

Katerina shrugged. "They are mostly peasants," she said. "If their parents died, then the lord could make them leave. They are too young and weak to work in the fields. Sometimes if they cannot get an apprenticeship, their parents send them away to make a life elsewhere."

Susan gulped. This was not her time or her place. She clamped her mouth shut and turned her attention to the group.

She noticed Jason. He was bent over the blanket where the food was laid out. He rose with some in his hands and moved over to sit next to Susan. He nodded to Katerina but then showed Susan the meagre handful he held.

"There's some cheese here," he said. "That looks OK." He poked it with his finger. "The bread is so stale it snaps. There's no meat."

Susan looked at the offerings. She took a piece of the crumbly cheese and nibbled at it.

Watt sat next to Katerina, and they shared what he had brought.

As dusk dimmed the light in the clearing, the children's chatter died down. Grefin sat with his back against a tree. The children gathered around him.

"Tell us again, Grefin," one of them piped up.

He smiled and nodded. At first he slumped over a little, but as he began to talk, he straightened. His tiredness seemed to fall away, and his face became animated and joyous. The children leaned forward with rapt attention. Susan moved forward, too. Here was a chance to find out what was happening and why she was here.

CHAPTER 7
GREFIN'S STORY

It was two Sundays ago now that this all began for me. I was drawn to the crowd standing in the square of our village. It was the middle of the day. People should have been busy at their summer tasks, but there they stood in the square. And they were quiet, too. No noise. When a baby cried, it was quickly shushed.

I had been sent by my master to fetch more leather from the tanner, and he'd cuffed me across the head as well. That's what masters do to apprentices. But here was a crowd. Something interesting must be happening. I pushed through until I could hear. Then a bit farther until I could see—Nicholas.

You want to know what he looked like? Grefin looked around at the gathered children.

The children nodded, rapt.

Hmmm, he was just a bit taller than me. He stood at the foot of our holy rood before our little church. His limbs were straight, and he held himself proudly. Dark hair, he had—longish. And his nose was the nose of an eagle. His eyes. Yes, his eyes. Sometimes they were a quiet blue, and then at other times, when he spoke, they blazed bluer than the bluest sky.

His voice was quite low and raspy. He swallowed a lot while he spoke. But his words—his words rang like church bells into our ears.

He spoke of Jesus Christ's holy city, Jerusalem, of the wonders of the place and of all the other things we hear about the holy land. How wonderful they are and how they are held in the grip of invaders.

He talked of the popes, one after the other, and how they had called for the knights of all Christian lands to ride to the rescue of our holy lands. How it was the duty of our soldiers and knights to drive the infidel from the streets of Jerusalem.

Then he lowered his voice, so we all had to strain to hear. He talked of the failure of the mighty. How kings and even queens had ridden to free the holy land and failed. He talked of their deaths, destruction, of their soldiers dying of disease and of their wounds. It had all been a complete failure. The infidel reigned supreme in Jerusalem.

Old Mother Agnes standing next to me began to sob quietly. Others were sniffing, and I saw that Hard Old Will, the blacksmith, was dabbing at his eyes with his sweat rag.

But Nicholas wasn't finished. He told us what the popes had promised the kings and their knights. Riding to the liberation of Jerusalem was a sacred duty, they said. These heroes, they said, were holy pilgrims and protected by God's hand. All their sins forgiven, all their afterlives blessed in the wonders of heaven.

But they failed, Nicholas told us. Even so they failed. Nicholas shook his head.

We all shook our heads, too.

Then Nicholas laid out his plan.

Innocent children would succeed where the mighty had failed. We would be the holy pilgrims and travel to Jerusalem.

Many in the crowd shook their heads and looked around at the children standing among them. Mothers clutched their children to their sides.

But Nicholas kept talking, and we kept listening.

We, the innocent children, would travel to Jerusalem, not with swords in our hands or hatred in our hearts. We would go as Christian pilgrims, and when the infidels saw our joyous devotion, they would be moved to become Christians as well. Then and only then would Jerusalem be free.

But how will we get there? I asked him. Grefin nodded. *I did.*

God will provide, he told me back. And I could see it. I could.

We would be the ones. What heroes we would be.

Many of the adults left the group then, shaking their heads and quietly talking among themselves. Many mothers dragged their children along with them.

But my master had entered the square. Looking for me, I suppose. He cuffed me a good one and yelled for me to get along. Shoes don't make themselves—he always said that. So I ran off to the tanners to get the leather I'd been sent for.

I kept thinking about what Nicholas had said, though, and as we bedded down for the night under the workbenches, I whispered to Oscar, the other apprentice, everything I heard.

He wanted to see Nicholas for himself, and he dragged me along with him. We crept out and hurried down the darkening street toward the square. We thought he would be staying somewhere close to the church.

As we drew closer, we saw a small fire in the corner of the churchyard under the branches of the oak tree that grew there. We followed the path. We saw that Nicholas was sitting cross-legged on the ground, talking to an adult who was sitting with his back against the tree. They talked quietly but stopped when they heard us approaching.

Nicholas beckoned us forward, and we were happy to join him.

He introduced us to his father. He was traveling with him.

I told Nicholas that I had heard his speech in the square and believed what he said to be true. He nodded and smiled at me. What a smile. It was like a light shone through him and illuminated my entire life. Oscar wasn't so sure, but I was. I knew I could follow that smile all the way to Jerusalem.

I asked him what I could do to start. He told me that he was traveling through the countryside, telling people his story, and that children who wished to join him should gather others to them.

He was planning to be in Cologne in mid-July and that others he had spoken to were out gathering other children to them, and they were all meeting in the great city of Cologne at that time.

And that's where we are all going now. We are on the road to Cologne. Then you will see Nicholas for yourselves and see that our pilgrimage is holy. We are just children, but I believe we will prevail in Jerusalem.

CHAPTER 8

HAIR

By the time Grefin had finished his story, it was almost dark, and many of the children were snuggled up, asleep.

Others pulled blankets around themselves and curled up where they were. Someone threw more wood on the little fires. The little camp of children settled down to sleep.

Jason tugged at Susan's arm. He beckoned with his head toward the trees, and Susan stood. They moved quietly toward the edge of the clearing and slipped along a little pathway. Susan heard a murmuring stream ahead, and they emerged from the trees to find a stream at their feet.

Quickly Jason grabbed Susan's shoulder, and the two crouched there. They could hear voices.

"But, my lady, your hair?" It was Watt talking. "Your grandmother will never forgive me."

"Do it, Watt. I command you." That was Katerina.

Jason jerked. He made a funny grunting sound. Susan looked to see what had happened, but he shook his head and waved toward the other two.

Susan and Jason crept a little closer.

Katerina sat on a rock by the stream. Watt stood behind her with a knife in his hand.

"Do it," Katerina insisted.

Susan jumped to her feet and rushed out of hiding. "Wait, wait, nothing is worth dying like that for. You don't have to marry that awful Sir Gustaff. You can get away from him. Marry someone else."

Katerina sprang to her feet. She scowled down at Susan. "What by the saints are you talking about?" she exclaimed. "You're spying on us," she added. Then she stamped her foot. Angry. Hands on hips. Deep frown on her face.

"Um." Susan looked down at her feet for a moment. "Watt had a knife. He was standing behind you. He didn't want to do it," Susan finished.

Jason, still clutching her arm, spoke. "It was Susan trying to save you," he offered.

"Huh." Katerina sat back on the stone. "And you think that I was running away from that oaf Gustaff because I was supposed to marry him?" She started to laugh.

Surprised, Susan turned to Jason. "You spoke," she said, "they understood you."

Jason grinned. "If I'm touching you, I can understand. I understood what they were saying because I had my hand on your shoulder." He chuckled. "I was very surprised."

Katerina raised one eyebrow. "What language is that you speak?" Watt moved up beside her and still held his knife out.

"Quick, grab my hand." Susan held hers out, and Jason grasped it.

"That is English," she said. "We come to your shores from very far away."

"Hmph, spies." Katerina scowled. "You helped me. Why?"

Susan shrugged. "You needed help." To change the subject, Susan asked, "So, what is happening here? Why is Watt, your friend, waving a knife around your head?"

Katerina smoothed her skirt over her knees. "I need to fit in better. These children are mostly peasants. No other girl has hair as long as mine. I need to travel with them. They hide me. Only lords and ladies can have hair this long. I must cut it. Watt must cut it for me." Then Katerina looked again at Susan. "Your hair is way too short. Have you been sick?"

Susan laughed. "That is way too long a story to tell. Here," she said as she rummaged in her bag. "I can help." She dug deeper. "I will cut your hair for you." Susan continued to run her hand through the objects in her bag. "I have them in here somewhere."

Finally, Susan pulled out a small pair of folding scissors. *Thank you, Mrs. Coleman*, she thought. She unfolded them carefully and moved behind Katerina to begin the job. But Katerina had noticed what Susan held and put her hand out for them. Susan handed them over.

"These are strange," Katerina said. "I have seen scissors before, but never so tiny or so fine." Katerina stroked them with her finger.

"Yes," Susan said firmly as she picked them from Katerina's hand. "Mr. Steel, the blacksmith in our village, is a fine craftsman."

Susan carefully began cutting into the thick black braids. She held them in her hands rather than letting them fall onto the grass at their feet. As she snipped, Katerina covered her face with her hands. Susan could only imagine how long it had taken to grow her hair so that it reached almost to her waist. She remembered how she had felt when she discovered her head had been shaved in Egypt, and she felt sorry for Katerina and the predicament she was in.

Once the braids were cut away, Susan handed them to Watt and began to tidy the hair and cut it into some sort of shape around her face and over her ears. Sometimes she had cut Judy's bangs for her, and for a moment, Susan felt such a pang of homesickness that she wanted to just leap home, but she continued to snip.

Jason sidled up beside her. "The hair is cut pretty rough here. Nobody is off to the salon for a hair styling."

He was right. Susan stopped cutting. She ruffled and fluffed Katerina's thick black hair. "That will be easier to keep clean and tidy on the road now," she said to Katerina.

Katerina stood stiffly and brushed down her skirt. "It had to be done," was all she said.

The four walked back to the clearing together. Jason cast around until he found a suitable spot. He beckoned Susan over. "This will work the best. It's a long time since I've slept on the ground like this." He ran his hands over the grass and plucked out a couple of pebbles. He sighed. "We used to go camping a lot before I got sick." He sprawled on his back. "I'd forgotten what it was like to feel healthy." He sighed. "Just look at those stars. No light pollution. They're wonderful."

Susan picked a spot on the grass next to him. "What a day."

Jason nodded. "It's great about the language. Finally I'll be able to understand what's happening."

Susan lay back. *Harsheer was a better magician than I thought.* She chuckled. *Or maybe it was Ma-at's finger in the mixture.*

"What do you think is up with Katerina—Miss I'm-Better-Than-You? Why is she hiding with us peasants?" Jason used air quotes on the last word.

Susan turned on her side. "Somehow it seems more like she's running *to* something than running *from* something."

"Well, we know at least three knights are looking for her."

Susan nodded. "I think we've found our adventure. I would never have thought we would be going on a pilgrimage."

"Oh, yeah, what was that story all about? I hadn't figured out about touching you yet."

"Tomorrow, tomorrow. I'll tell you while we're walking. We'll be doing a lot of walking."

Jason settled to sleep. "Good night," he murmured.

Susan was too near sleep to answer him.

CHAPTER 9

ON THE ROAD

The day began early. Even before the sun came up, the chill in the air and the dew had awakened Susan and Jason. Most of the other children were stirring, too. Grefin poked a few sticks into the embers of the fire, and they all huddled around, holding their hands to the heat.

There was hardly any food, but a few pieces of crumbling cheese were shared out. Susan stopped Jason from taking a share of the cheese, and they started out a little ahead of the group.

The walking warmed them. They set a brisk pace along the path until they were well ahead of the rest. As they walked, Susan retold Grefin's story for Jason.

"We're walking to Jerusalem!" Jason sat quickly on the side of the track.

Susan joined him and delved into her bag for a granola bar. "Do you really think these children will make it to Jerusalem?" She stared at the path ahead. "Maybe I'm supposed to convince them to go home."

"Seems more sensible." Jason bit into his bar with relish.

Susan chewed and swallowed. "Yes, but Katerina called them peasants, and even though she's traveling with them and hiding among them, she doesn't seem to have much respect for them. So maybe this seems like a good choice for these children—young as they are.

"We're going to Cologne first," Susan informed him. "We're meeting up with someone called Nicholas there. According to Grefin, there are children gathering from all over, and then they're off to Jerusalem."

Jason shook his head. "Seems a bit harebrained."

Susan agreed. "Seems desperate to me. These children have nothing."

"Yep." Jason stood and dusted off his pants. "Cologne. I've heard of that place. There still is a Cologne, I think. I bet we're in Germany—or maybe France."

Susan shrugged. "Whichever, it's a long way to Jerusalem." She gathered the foil and paper and carefully folded them back into her bag.

Jason watched her.

"It's not of this time," she explained. "Who knows what trouble it could cause if we left it lying around."

Jason wriggled his fingers. "Oooh yes, we could be accused of witchcraft or something."

"And that wouldn't be funny," Susan retorted. "They used to burn witches at the stake. Men and women, boys and girls."

"You're right." Jason sighed. "Everything is so different. Makes you realize how far we've come in the years between here and our time."

"Huh." Susan put her head to one side. "It's not exactly like that. It's not a smooth, steady rise. I was in Egypt, and that was way further back in time than this, and it was more civilized back there than it is here, I think. People weren't ragged or starving. They smiled and danced and sang."

⊨+ +⊨

Loud coughing heralded the arrival of the pilgrim children. Grefin was carrying one of the smaller children on his hip. The child's face was flushed red, and she looked miserable. Her bare little feet flapped listlessly against Grefin's leg as he walked along.

Grefin flopped down alongside Susan and laid the little girl carefully on the grassy verge. "She is so ill." He shook his head sadly. "Her sister died yesterday, just before you joined us, and now little Petriona is coughing just the same way." He smoothed back the hair from her forehead.

Jason leaned over the girl and touched her face carefully with his hand. "She has a fever. We need to bring her temperature down," he said. "Susan, wet a rag and put it on her forehead." Jason looked up at Grefin. "We need to get some good, nourishing food into her." He surveyed the group standing, watching. "We could all do with some good food."

Grefin looked at Jason, puzzled. Susan hurried over and placed her hand on Jason's shoulder. "Say it again." She laughed.

Jason sighed. "I've got to learn the language," he said and then repeated what he had already said.

Grefin took it from there. He had the girls search out a stream for some water. He sent some of the larger boys into the fields with their slingshots to search for game. Others built a fire and set a pot ready for water. Digging among the shrubbery along the side of the track, one girl pulled up a root, which she held high. Others joined her, laughing, and found more. *Maybe they're wild onions,* Susan hoped.

Katerina and Watt stood and watched for a while.

Out of the corner of her eye, Susan watched Katerina become more and more agitated as time went on. *She wants to leave.*

Susan was right. Katerina set off, hurrying along the path on her own. Watt chased after her, and the two stood for a while. Watt spoke, and Katerina listened, folding her arms and shaking her head. Watt waved back toward the group and continued talking.

I wish I could hear what they're saying, Susan thought.

But her main concern was Petriona. As soon as water arrived, Susan began bathing the little girl's face.

Petriona sighed and lay relaxed on the grass. Susan tried to open her clothing to cool the little girl further. There were no buttons. Petriona was sewn into her coat. A quick yank opened the stitching, and Susan was able to fold back the edges. This exposed just how pitifully thin the little girl was. Susan could see the bump of each rib.

Susan continued to bathe the little girl with cool water. Petriona sighed again and slipped into a quiet sleep. Susan then had time to look around and see what else was happening.

First she noticed that Katerina and Watt had returned to the group. Katerina stood frowning by the fire. Watt busied himself cutting the roots the girls had found.

The children had made camp. Even though it was early in the day, they had fires lit and water boiled in the little pot. One of the boys arrived, holding a duck aloft. "I got one," he cried. "I found the perfect stone. I whirled my slingshot, and I got one."

Grefin sighed. "The Lord has provided," he said. And then he went to work plucking and gutting the bird. He popped the meat into the boiling water.

Jason came over to check on Petriona. He dropped down beside Susan.

"That was interesting," he said. "I went with them. Couldn't understand a word they said but I saw what they did. I need a slingshot, I think."

Susan nodded. "It would be a good idea to learn the language, too. That way we don't have to always be touching."

Jason looked down at Petriona.

"Quick," he started. "She's shivering. We need to get her warmer now."

Susan quickly closed the little coat around the whimpering girl. She grabbed her up and hugged her to her to chest. Susan pulled her coat around the two of them to keep in the heat.

Jason jumped up and ran to Katerina where she was standing by the fire. He grabbed her cloak from around her shoulders and hurried back toward Susan.

"This is about the warmest thing here," he said as he bundled Petriona into the cloak.

In the warmth, Petriona relaxed again. She sighed once and slipped into sleep.

"Sleep's the best thing for her." Jason nodded gravely. He felt her forehead. "She feels about normal now."

Susan sat back with a sigh. "How do you know all this stuff about fevers?" she asked.

Jason shrugged. "Live in a hospital as much as I have and you learn a bit about it all. How many fevers do you think I've had over the years?"

Susan nodded. Seeing Jason as he was now, she had almost forgotten the sickly boy who had arrived at their house just a month before. *Well—a month and a few hundred years.* Susan chuckled to herself.

Most of the group had gathered around the fire. All staring at the pot. Watching the meat and vegetables slowly cook into stew. A wonderful smell wafted from the pot. All attention was on the bubbling food.

That's when it happened.

Hard hands grabbed Susan's arm. Jason was flattened with one blow. Susan screamed and thrashed her hand out, but it was too late. She was sitting and had no leverage to protect herself.

The three knights were back. Quietly. Without their horses.

CHAPTER 10
THE KNIGHTS

A t Susan's scream, the children scattered. They ran into the forest. The third knight had a firm hold on Watt.

"See, see," he crowed. "I knew this was the stable groom. I knew it."

Sir Gustaff sauntered over until he was towering over Watt. "Yes, yes, Sir Klaus, we heard you the first time."

He bent until his face was right next to Watt's. "Now. You. Where's Katerina? Tell me quick." He lifted his hand high and smacked Watt across the cheek.

Watt's head rocked back, and he would have fallen if the other knight hadn't held him tight. Susan had never heard such a horrible scrunching sound before, and she never wanted to hear it again. She gulped and tried to shake her arm free from the knight holding her.

"Be still," he whispered. "There is nothing you can do to help him now."

Susan turned to her captor. "Sir Robert?" When he nodded, she continued. "Why are you doing this? These children are holy pilgrims. Misguided maybe but they're not hurting you or doing any harm."

"We must find the Lady Katerina." Sir Robert gestured at the blue cloak wrapped around Petriona. "You have her cloak." He nodded to where Watt and Sir Gustaff stood. "Watt was the groom who tended her horse."

Sir Gustaff delivered another glancing blow to Watt's head. The same sound again. Sir Gustaff—the oaf—wore a mail glove over his hand. Blood flowed freely down the side of Watt's face. Susan shuddered.

Sir Robert continued. "We must find her. She is a lady. A royal lady. She is in great danger. She disappeared from the villa at the same time as that boy. We must be sure he doesn't know where she is."

Susan turned and looked squarely at Sir Robert. "Yes," she sneered. "Beating Watt senseless will really help. He'll really want to help you find her now."

Sir Robert looked down his nose at her. "You have her cloak." He shook her. "What do you know?"

Susan hoped her dismay didn't show on her face. "I told you what I know," she said. "A lady gave me her cloak. Was I supposed to say no thank you?" She stroked the collar. "It's a lovely cloak."

"Indeed, it is." Sir Robert nodded. "I gifted it to her last Michaelmas. And now here it is, dirty, wrapped around a filthy peasant child, and where is Katerina?"

Susan gulped. She could see Katerina over Sir Robert's shoulder. She was lying in the bushes a few feet away. Tears tracked down her cheeks.

I have to stop this. Susan looked around for anything that might give her an idea of what she could do.

Jason groaned and began to pull himself up into a sitting position. He had one hand holding his head where Sir Gustaff had hit him on his way into the group.

He looks awful, Susan worried. *I can't have him leaping into the fight and getting sick again.*

She turned to Sir Robert, trying to stay calm. She hoped he couldn't hear her heart hammering. She made her voice small, and she didn't need to try to sound afraid.

"Oh, sir," she quavered. "The lady made me promise not to tell." She put her hand up as though to ward off a blow.

"The lady is in danger. You must tell me." Sir Robert quieted his voice. "Tell me what you know."

Susan took a big breath and prepared to tell the biggest whopper of her life.

"Well, kind sir," she said. "The lady came the same day as that boy over there." She waved her arm toward Watt. "They were arguing, like, and he was telling her to go back, but she was saying that she had to get to the...erm..." Susan looked around. Where was the most unlikely place that Katerina might have wanted to go? "The sea," she blurted out. "Yes." She nodded. "The sea, she wanted to go to the sea."

Sir Robert looked puzzled. "Did she say why?"

Susan shook her head. "But she wanted to hurry. She wanted my cloak. She said it was a better dis-dis..." Susan deliberately stumbled over the word.

"Disguise?" Sir Robert asked.

Susan nodded again. *I'm getting too good at this.* Jason was watching her with his mouth open.

"Tell me what your cloak looked like," Sir Robert said.

"Well." Susan drew it out. She put her finger to her chin. "It was the color of that tree trunk over there," Susan said, pointing across the clearing. "It had a lovely deep hood that I could pull down way over my face. My sisters all wore it before me. But it was mine now. The lady wanted it."

Susan looked around the clearing. Everyone was watching her. Watt hung limp in the hands of Sir Klaus. Sir Gustaff was pacing back and forth, punching his fist into his other hand. They were all listening. Grefin stood by the bubbling stewpot, his mouth gaping.

Susan took a deep breath. *Now what?*

Sir Robert solved that question. "But if she's not here, where is she?"

Susan shrugged to give herself time to think. "Um. She went the other way," she said.

"Along the road?" Sir Gustaff strode over and stood, glowering down.

Susan shook her head. "For a bit," she said. "I looked back, and I saw her take a little path that led into the forest." She shook her head. "Then I didn't see her."

Sir Klaus dropped Watt onto the grass. "Come on," he said. "We have to catch her. All is lost if we don't catch her soon."

Sir Gustaff turned on his heel and strode out of the clearing. But on his way, he snarled and kicked over the stewpot. All the food spilled into the fire and on the ground.

Sir Robert rose from his spot next to Susan and walked over to Watt. "For your trouble," he said and dropped a tinkling purse at Watt's feet.

As he walked after the other two, Susan heard him say, "I thought she loved me. She always seemed happy. Why would she run away?" He was shaking his head.

As soon as the knights disappeared along the path, everyone in the clearing seemed able to move again. Grefin quickly tried to retrieve as much of the cooked duck as he could. Jason hurried to Watt's side. Petriona took that moment to awaken. Soon her wracking coughs were the loudest noise in the clearing.

Susan sat slumped in place, allowing herself to shake all over now that the crisis was past.

CHAPTER 11
BESIDE THE CREEK

Jason put his arm around Susan's shoulders. "You were great. How did you think up all that stuff?"

"I was soooo scared," was all Susan could say. "How is Watt?"

Jason shrugged. "He seems OK. Better than I thought he would be after those hits he took." Jason shook his head. "Can you believe how those knights acted? Talk about knight brutality. I thought knights were supposed to be all noble and protecting of people."

"So did I." Susan looked around. "Where is he?"

"I told him to go down to the creek to wash the wound on his head and to rinse off some of the blood on his clothes." Jason grinned. "He probably wants to count the money in that purse Sir Robert threw him."

Susan rose shakily to her feet. "We better check on him to make sure he's all right."

Jason jumped up, too. "Oops, I forgot about concussion. We better check."

The two hurried down to the creek. Watt sat on the bank with his feet in the water. He was using a cloth to bathe the cut on his head. Jason hurried over to him. "I need to look at your eyes, Watt." He knelt down beside him and gently took his head into his hands.

Susan looked along the creek. She hadn't had time to come down to the water before. It looked like a peaceful place. But such violence had occurred just a few steps away. On this side of the creek, there was a little grassy clearing. Most of the creek bed was covered in smooth, worn pebbles, but two larger mossy stones stuck out of the shallow water.

On the other side of the creek, tall trees grew right down to the water's edge. It was difficult to see into the forest because the shrubs growing around the base of the trees were so thick.

Susan was thinking about kneeling down to scoop a drink of the clear water when she heard a big sniff and what sounded like a stifled sob.

Susan looked up quickly. *Who?*

Katerina sat a little back from the trees on the edge of the clearing. She was slumped forward over her lap, her head on her knees. Her tousled, short hair stood up in spikes. Susan noticed a small leaf nestled by her ear.

Susan heard another big sniff. She saw that Katerina had a fold of paper in one hand.

Susan sighed and walked over to the sobbing girl.

"Can I help?" she asked softly.

Katerina gave a big sniff and turned away.

"Sometimes it helps to talk about what is troubling you," Susan suggested.

"You can't help me," Katerina murmured. "No one can help me."

"Hey, I've helped you already. I just sent the nasty knights on a wild goose chase in the opposite direction. They obviously want to catch you, but I don't think it's for your own good or anything."

Katerina sighed. "They're not all nasty," she said and began sobbing loudly.

"Look, you obviously don't want them to catch you. You've run away from something. You're wandering along, hiding in a straggle of children who are so lost they think they're going to walk to Jerusalem to convert the infidels. There is nothing you can tell me that would make this situation any weirder than it already is."

Katerina turned to Susan. "That's all true, but I have to get to Cologne as soon as I can. It's important to my family. It's important to the entire Holy Roman Empire. I have to get to Cologne."

Susan took a moment. *The Holy Roman Empire—where's that? This isn't how Romans dress, is it?*

"That Sir Robert said you were a royal lady. So why are you traveling with a bunch of children?

Katerina shook her head. "I don't know who else to trust."

Susan nodded wisely. "Yes, well, that can be a problem," she agreed. "But why are you crying now? You weren't before."

Katerina held out the paper in her hand. Susan took it from her. She couldn't read it. She handed it back.

"I can speak your language, but I can't read it," she said.

Katerina took the paper back and smoothed it over her knees. She smiled sadly as she looked down at the words written there.

"This letter was in the pouch with the coins that Robert threw to Watt. It's from Robert to me."

Susan gasped. "He knew you were there all the time?"

Katerina shook her head. "He hoped I was somewhere in contact with Watt. Let me read."

She began, "My dearest, sweet Kat." Katerina looked up quickly.

She's blushing, Susan noticed.

"Just tell me what it says," Susan suggested.

Katerina nodded and looked back down at the words. "He says he hopes I'm well. He says he doesn't understand why I ran away. He thought I was happy. He says that Gustaff and his father raged for half a day when they found I was gone. Soldiers have been sent to all their estates to warn their retainers that I must be found." Katerina stroked the paper with her little finger. "He says he loves me still. And that as far as he is concerned, we are betrothed now, even though we weren't going to make it official until Saint Swithin's Day."

Katerina used her sleeve to wipe the tears from her cheeks.

Susan watched her. She was obviously missing Robert and far from home and friends. But Susan could see bravery in the way she was carrying on with her rush to Cologne. It seemed to Susan that Katerina had left a comfortable life and people who loved her. Her secret must be important for her to be straggling down a dusty road with a bunch of children.

Susan waited a moment to let Katerina have time to fold up the letter and carefully tuck it into her bag.

"Well," Susan said. "Why did you leave in secret and such a rush?"

Katerina looked straight at her. "I have to get to Cologne as quickly as I can," she said. "I can't tell you why. It is a dangerous secret." She hammered her fist into her knee to emphasize her next words. "I. Have. To. Reach. Cologne."

Jason and Watt joined the two girls at that moment.

Watt looked less shaky on his feet, but the cut on his head looked deep and hadn't sealed up well. One side of his face already showed bruising.

"It doesn't look as though he has a concussion." Jason shook his head. "Pretty hardheaded. We'll have to watch him, though, to make sure. The mailed glove did that damage to his head."

Susan scrambled to her feet, and Jason leaned down and offered Katerina his hand to help her up.

The four hurried through the gathering dusk to the clearing where the children were huddled around a fire.

CHAPTER 12
MONEY

Grefin looked up from the firelight as the four entered the clearing.

"There is no food," he said. "Your Sir Gustaff kicked it into the fire."

Katerina lifted her head high. "He's not my Gustaff," she said. "He's an oaf and a bully."

The children all turned to look at the four. Several of the smaller children started to whimper, and one little one stuck his thumb in his mouth.

Grefin glared at Katerina. "True, but they are powerful in this physical world. We are holy pilgrims following a holy cause. We must follow our path to Cologne. They are searching for you, and that puts us all in danger."

Susan stepped forward. "That is true. They are searching for her, and you have been heroic to keep her here in your midst. I lied to the knights and sent them in the opposite direction. I don't think they will return." She spread her hands for peace. "We all want to get to Cologne."

Jason stepped up next to Susan and put his hand on her shoulder. "This day is over. Tomorrow is a new day," he said. "Hungry as we are, we will all feel better after a night's sleep." He looked at one of the other boys. "Ulric, didn't you set a couple of snares earlier?"

Ulric looked at Jason in surprise and nodded.

"There," said Jason. "Tomorrow there will be food. Tomorrow we will go forward." Then he turned and looked over to the area where Petriona lay. "It would be good if we could find some honey and some lemons tomorrow, too," he added. Then he walked over and sat beside Petriona.

After that, everyone settled down for sleep. The fire ebbed to a bed of glowing embers, and soon all was quiet in the clearing, except for the occasional cough or mutter.

⚔️

Susan woke early. Dew had settled on her shoulder, and the chilly air made her shiver. *We are going to need some supplies to continue in this time*, she thought.

She stood and began some slow stretching exercises to limber her muscles after a night of lying on the hard ground. It felt good to move slowly and gracefully in the quiet, stretching one set of muscles and then the next. But the actions reminded her of home. Often, she and her mum stretched like this out in the garden under the maple tree. Home. Family.

Susan looked around the clearing. Where were the homes and families of these children? Did they have homes and families? Susan shook her head. And what about Katerina? She obviously had a home, but something was wrong.

Hmm, maybe this is the wrong I am here to help with.

Susan lifted her arms way up above her head and slowly moved to the right, stretching the left side of her body. Then she did the same, moving to the left. To finish, she gave her hands a good shake. She looked around.

Breakfast would be good.

As if on cue, Jason and Ulric walked into the clearing, each holding up a dead rabbit. Both carried bloodied knives, and Susan saw that the rabbits had already been gutted but not skinned. The children began to stir. Grefin sent someone for water for the pot. An older girl began searching for roots to add to the meat. Food. There was excitement in the air.

Jason walked over to where Susan stood.

"I went to see how he set the snares," he said as he plunged the knife into the dirt. It came out clean.

"You seem to get on with everyone even without language." Susan nodded with approval.

"I'm picking up a few words." Jason shrugged. "I can't spend all my time with my hand on your shoulder."

"You've acquired a knife." Susan admired it. "It's better for this time than the Swiss Army knife I have in my bag."

Jason nodded. "Yep, genuine very old."

"How?"

Jason grinned. "Reagan had a spare one, from one of the children who died before we joined them. I've got some change in my pocket, and he took a quarter for it. He liked the silver. He said it looked like a thaler."

Surprised, Susan dug around in her bag. "I've got change, too." She pulled out a little purse and dragged out a handful of coins. "Mrs. Coleman has all sorts of coins in here. I guess some of them will do here. I wonder what they would think of a toonie?" She chuckled.

Watt joined them. "Did you catch the rabbit?" he asked. But his eyes found the coins in Susan's hand. "You are wealthy," he said.

Susan shook her head. "Not really. These coins aren't of here."

Watt shook his head. "That doesn't matter. A merchant weighs coins and decides what he will trade for each." Watt looked at them. "It's different in your land?" He gingerly picked up a quarter from Susan's hand. "Ah, this," he said, holding it up. "It's silver. There is a stag." He turned it over. "A queen, you have a queen?" He shook his head again. "She must be mighty."

Susan took the coin from his fingers and slipped it back into her purse with the others. "I guess the dollar notes aren't going to be much use," she said to Jason with a grin.

He grinned back. "Well, it looks as though we're rich enough to buy ourselves blankets and coats—and more food."

"If we ever get anywhere that we can," she agreed.

The aroma of roasting rabbit drifted over the little camp. Susan instantly felt every pang of hunger. Her feet followed her nose to the fireside.

Someone had skinned the rabbits and broken them into pieces. Each piece was skewered onto a green stick and held over the flames on a framework.

By the time the rabbit pieces began to sizzle, everyone was clustered around, all eyes riveted on the cooking meat. Slowly, too slowly, it all cooked. It could never be fast enough for the waiting children.

CHAPTER 13

MARKET DAY

With every scrap of food eaten and the pot washed in the stream, the children set out along the road again. Not all together but spread out. Each leaving when they were ready. Grefin lagged behind. He fussed around the camp, making sure all was as it should be and that nothing and nobody was left behind.

Susan shouldered her bag with a sigh and readied herself for another day of walking. Jason lifted Petriona to her feet and carefully folded the blue cloak. With food and rest, Petriona looked less flushed and was coughing less. Jason patted her back for encouragement and gently urged her to join the other children, but she clutched her little hand into the seam of his jeans and hung on tight.

Susan smiled at the sight. "Seems you have a fan there." She chuckled.

Jason smiled back. "Huh, fine, but I can't walk with a little girl attached to my leg." He gently pried Petriona's fingers from his pants and put her hand into the hand of another child just starting out.

Katerina and Watt walked by, and as they did so, Jason handed the blue cloak to Katerina with a slight bow.

"Thank you." Katerina looked surprised. Watt took the cloak from her hands and shook it out. Then he draped it carefully around her shoulders. They walked on, hurrying to catch up with the bulk of the children.

Susan shook her head. "There's a lot more story there," she said.

Jason nodded in agreement. He walked over to Grefin and helped him with the last of the cleanup. And then the three of them began the daily trudge together.

But this day was different. Many more people walked the road with them. Most carried bundles on their backs. Some trudged along; others walked with a light step and a smile for everyone. Many pushed handcarts piled high with vegetables and fruit. Only the people accompanied by children seemed wary of Grefin's bedraggled group.

"It's a market day," Grefin informed them and then hurried forward to herd his charges into a tighter group.

Susan and Jason acted as rear guard, so Susan had a good opportunity to observe these market people and their reactions to the children. She saw many cross themselves in a blessing as they passed. Others looked with scorn on the group. Most ignored the children as they hurried by.

One woman, burdened with a heavy sack across her shoulders, bent to Petriona and patted her head. She stroked her flushed cheeks and then moved on. Petriona looked with wonder at the fresh apple now nestled in her hand. She bit into it hungrily.

Susan also noticed Katerina's reaction to the crowded road. She pulled her hood well up over her head and huddled along. Watt hurried at her side, using his body to hide her even more.

They both look so furtive. They're attracting more attention that way. As she watched, Katerina and Watt slipped quietly off the road and into the woods. Susan nudged Jason in the shoulder, and they dropped back a little and then followed them into the trees.

Jason and Susan found the two of them sheltering behind the trunk of a large tree. They were arguing in whispers, but their body language was loud with anger.

Watt: "We need to stay among the children. It's our best cover."

Katerina: "I can't go into that town. People have known me there. I'll be recognized."

Watt: "Humph. Unlikely. Have you thought what you look like now? My lady?"

Katerina: "Yes, I have. I don't want to be seen like this. I would bring shame on my family. Someone will recognize me. I don't know who to trust."

"Ahem." Susan and Jason walked quietly around the tree trunk. "Sorry, couldn't help overhearing." She patted Katerina's arm. "Why can't you be seen? What is going on? We can probably help."

Katerina turned her haughty back. "I have to get to Cologne."

Susan shrugged. "Uh-huh. You said that. Standing behind a tree, arguing, isn't getting you there."

Katerina whirled around to face her. "Neither will being recognized in the town." Katerina flapped her hands. "It's market day. Everyone will be out and about in the streets. I'll be spotted—and recognized." Katerina hung her head.

"So?"

Katerina sighed. Her shoulders slumped. "Even if they can be trusted, people will talk. I cut my hair off. I'm dirty, but I am still me, and I will be recognized." She shook her head. "That must not be. In Cologne I will be safe."

Watt stood by during this conversation, but his eyes continually scanned the area. He was watchful and ready for action. Jason nudged Susan's shoulder and jerked his head in that direction. "I bet Watt's a soldier."

"No, he's a page in my cousin's court," Katerina answered.

Susan and Jason both looked at her, open-mouthed. "You understood?"

"My betrothed is English. Sir Robert is an Englishman. I am learning. I recognized the word soldier. You have horrible accents."

Susan laughed. "Everybody says everyone else has an accent."

Katerina puffed out a breath. "You use many, many words that I have never heard," she said.

"Ain't that straight up?" Jason nodded.

"See, see, not one of those words made sense." Katerina stabbed the air with her finger.

Susan sat and leaned against the tree. All but Watt joined her, sitting in a tight group.

Katerina smiled up at Watt's back. "He was sent to fetch me. My cousin charged him with my protection. Frederick thought that a young person would have more chance of being able to blend in at the fortress."

Susan nodded. "OK." Then she laughed.

Jason looked at her sideways.

"I think I have the solution," she said.

Even Watt turned to hear what she had to say.

Susan began. "Even though you've got short hair now, your clothes are of such good quality that you still stand out."

Katerina spread her hands. "I have no others," she said.

Susan nodded. "It's market day. We can get you something there that will help you blend in better."

Katerina sighed. "I suppose. I have others in Cologne." She looked at Susan. "But how? I can't go among the people there."

Susan smiled at her. "You and I are about the same size. I will get you something that will fit—oh, better still, we'll get you something that doesn't fit well."

Jason waved his arms around his head. "Yes, and one of those huge straw hats that some of the farmer ladies wear."

It was soon arranged. Katerina dug into her bag and pulled out a handful of coins, which she gave to Watt. Jason was disappointed about missing the market but agreed to wait with Katerina. They could hide in the forest. Susan would walk into the market with Watt.

"Get lots to eat," Jason said as they prepared to leave.

Susan laughed and nodded.

Watt bowed formally to Katerina. "I will return shortly, my lady," he said gravely.

"Godspeed," Katerina called after them as they walked away. The two, Watt and Susan, hurried along the road, eager to reach the market.

───

It's just like a farmers market, was Susan's first thought upon entering the town square. People bustled everywhere. Farmers sat on little folding stools close to their spread-out wares. Some sellers stood beside their handcarts and sold directly from there.

And the buyers, carrying large baskets and bags, moved from seller to seller, squeezing the fruit and sniffing the vegetables. *Except for the clothes, this could be our farmers market at home,* Susan thought as she swiveled her head, trying to see everything at once.

And then a troubadour strummed his guitar and started to sing. *So much like home.* Susan chuckled.

Watt tugged her arm and pulled her over to a table where a woman sat with a wide array of clothing. A couple of dresses were spread on the table, but most of the clothes were jumbled in two large boxes. Susan started picking through the nearest one. The stuff was pretty bad. It had all been worn before, and a lot of it smelled of old, old sweat. Susan wrinkled her nose and kept digging.

71

Near the bottom Susan's fingers brushed against a softer fabric. She hauled out a brown dress. It looked pretty clean. She held it up to herself. She could fit into it—if there were two of her. She shook it out. Maybe a belt would make it work. They could roll up the sleeves. Susan turned to see what Watt thought and saw that he was elbow-deep in the other box. He held up a pair of pants, measuring them against his waist.

Susan gave a hoot. "That's it." She laughed. "It worked for me on the ship." She moved to Watt's side. "I think Katerina just became Karl," she said, taking the pants from him. She held them up to herself and wriggled her eyebrows.

Watt snatched them back. "It would be too improper." He shook his head.

Susan snatched them again. "She wants to get to Cologne," she said, shaking the pants in front of him. "Watt, she's in a hurry. She can't be discovered. Who would ever expect Lady High Mucky-Muck to be traveling disguised as a boy?"

Watt scratched his head. "She will never agree."

"It's the best solution," Susan argued. "Find a top that will go with these pants."

Watt burrowed back into the bin, shaking his head. He pulled out a tunic, held it up to himself. Raised his eyebrows in a question. Susan shook her head.

He sighed and threw it back. The next tunic he drew from the bin was a donkey-brown color with long sleeves. It was big and hung down almost to Watt's knees. Susan took it in her hands and sniffed it. Not too bad. She sniffed again. There was a vague scent of mint. She nodded. "This one," she said.

Watt shook his head. "It's too big."

"That's the idea. There's some curves she has that we need to hide."

Susan spotted a red scarf. "This will work for a belt."

Watt turned to a basket of leather. "Men—and even boys—wear a leather belt so they can hang things on it." He waved his hand at his own belt and swaggered in a circle.

Susan grinned to herself. *Boys.*

Watt paid for the clothing but not the first price asked. The table owner drove a hard bargain, but so did Watt. Back and forth, they dickered until a deal was struck.

Susan watched. *More like a flea market than a farmers market*, she thought.

With the clothes in a bundle, Watt set off across the square, ready to return to the forest.

Susan stood her ground. Watt turned back to see where she was. He beckoned. She shook her head. He turned and continued walking. Susan stood.

Reluctantly Watt returned to Susan.

"What?" he asked.

"Food," she said.

Watt shrugged. "Once she's a boy, we can come in and get food together."

"For the children," Susan said and hurried over to one of the stalls heaped with vegetables.

Watt sighed and followed. "They'll get plenty from the people in the town. They're pilgrims."

"They're thin and sickly and need better food." Susan looked back over her shoulder. "Well, actually they need everything. Shoes, coats, blankets. Toys. They're children, and they don't have toys." She shook her head. "Food. That's what they need most." Susan was determined.

"Don't know how you're going to carry it," Watt muttered.

"Let me worry about that," Susan retorted. "Just help me find stuff that will last and that they can eat. I know that Jason also needs to eat a lot more than he has been. He's always hungry."

Gradually they gathered foodstuffs from the tables. Susan selected. Watt bargained. They found some dried meat. They bought several dried fish. Susan sniffed the fish doubtfully, but Watt said it was fine. They accumulated fruit, too. Oranges, plums, grapes, lemons. The lemons reminded Susan about a soother for Petriona's cough, so they hunted out a little pot of honey.

Lastly they were drawn to a table selling freshly baked bread. The smell drifted over the market square, and many people clustered around the baker's table. Watt pushed through the crowd and returned with several loaves of bread warm in his fingers. But Susan had noticed a wonderful cake sitting on the side of the table. Fruit cake, studded with raisins, nuts…Susan sniffed the air. She imagined that she could smell the rich aroma of the cake.

"We need that, too." Susan pointed to the cake. Watt grunted, dived back into the crowd, and soon emerged again with the cake.

"Can we go now?" Watt asked, exasperated. He looked at Susan standing there, her arms full of their purchases. "How are you going to walk with all that stuff?"

Susan just smiled. "Help me a moment," she said and off-loaded the pile into Watt's outstretched arms.

Then she dug in her bag. *Thank you, Mrs. Coleman*, she thought and pulled out a long length of material. She spread it on a vacant table. "Put all the food on there," she said.

Watt shrugged and dumped all their purchases onto the cloth. Then he bent down to pick up the pieces he'd dropped. You don't shrug when your arms are full of food. Standing again he watched in wonder as Susan grasped two opposite corners of the cloth and pulled them tight over the food. She tied a knot and let the ends dangle. Then she grabbed the other two corners and pulled them over the food as well. She tied a double knot this time, making sure it was secure. She picked up the dangling ends and pulled them up and tied a knot in the very top.

Susan picked up the bundle and hitched it over Watt's shoulder. The bundle hung against his hip. Susan cocked her head and smiled. "Let's go," she said.

CHAPTER 14

THE HOLY ROMAN
EMPIRE

And they went. Heading back along the road to Katerina and Jason.

As they trudged, Susan kept her eye out for any of the children from Grefin's group, but it seemed that they had already passed the town, pushing along toward Cologne.

Many other children walked the road, though. She watched them carefully and was surprised at the differences they showed. Some clusters slogged along, heads down, shoulders slumped, just putting one foot in front of the other. Another group they passed was jubilant. Some children danced with light steps, singing praises, laughing and smiling.

But for all their differences, she noticed similarities as well. Poorly dressed, thin, dirty. Bigger children cared for the younger, smaller ones. All heading to Cologne to hear Nicholas tell them about how they would free Jerusalem without a fight.

Susan saw Watt shake his head. He looked grim.

"You were one of these children when we first saw you," she told him.

Watt turned to look at her as they walked. "We were hiding among them," he said.

"We've got a walk ahead of us. Tell me about it," Susan offered.

Watt smiled. "You're the curious one, aren't you?" He tugged gently at a tuft of her hair. "No hair to speak of, outlandish clothes, speaking all languages, obviously a stranger in our land, just a child really, and yet, so confident."

Susan looked at him from under her eyelashes. "Are you dodging the question?"

Watt shook his head. "It's not all my story to tell."

"Secrets, secrets. Tired of secrets." Susan poked him in the ribs. "Tell me how you ended up in the princess's—or whatever she is—company."

"She's not a princess, but she is a royal lady and well connected," Watt began. "She was fostered with the family of Sir Gustaff. They're Welfs, and she's Hohenstaufen."

"And that means something?" Susan wanted to know.

"Yes, it means a lot." Watt sighed. "Let me explain."

"That would be good. Start at the beginning, please. I'm a stranger here, you know." *In more ways than one*, Susan added to herself.

Watt began. "We are walking in the Holy Roman Empire. It is made up of lots of small realms, which are controlled by kings, dukes, or nobles. Each rules over their own territory, but they get together and elect an overall leader from among themselves, and this person becomes the Holy Roman emperor, blessed by the pope and with overall control of a country that stretches from the Baltic Sea to well into Italy."

Susan nodded. "It's sort of like a democracy."

Watt looked puzzled. "What's that?"

"Never mind." Susan waved her hand. "Continue, please. Tell me about these Welfs and the Hoh-Hohfens—you know what I mean."

Watt laughed. "For many years now, the Welf family and the Hohenstaufen have been wrestling over who would be the emperor. First one family would be in power, then a death or a revolution or an assassination, and then the other would be in power. A year or so ago, Otto was crowned emperor by the pope. He's a Welf. He became Otto IV. The Hohenstaufen king, who many thought should be emperor, was only a young boy at the time. He's actually king of Sicily, which is a long way away from here. His name is Frederick."

Susan ticked off the points on her fingers. "So you've got an emperor, Otto, and King Frederick is miles and miles away in Sicily. So everything is peaceful—right?"

Watt laughed and shook his head. "Many people hoped so, but it was not to be." He thumped his chest with a closed fist. "I serve Frederick, king of Sicily. He is my liege lord." He nodded to Susan as if to say, "So there."

Susan caught his arm and stopped Watt from walking farther. "I'm pretty sure this is where we came out of the forest onto the road," she said, peering into the trees. "Jason and Katerina should be just through there." Susan hitched up her bag, checked that the road was clear, and slipped among the trees.

Watt took the time to loosen his knife in his belt and then hurried after her.

"Wait," he whispered. "They should have been watching for us."

Susan instantly realized her mistake. She crouched down, and Watt joined her low in the bushes.

In the quiet, Susan heard a quiet snuffling sound, as though someone were crying quietly. Watt dropped the bag of food, pulled his knife, and crept as quietly as possible through the bushes toward the sound. Susan followed, carefully placing each footstep.

Jason lay in the little clearing. Flat on his back, with his legs stretched out straight and his arms folded onto his chest, he lay too still. Susan's heart leaped into her throat and then sank to her feet as she fell to her knees. *What will I tell Uncle John and Aunt Laura?*

Watt gently helped Susan to her feet. "Come," he said. "Let's see what has befallen."

The two walked quietly into the clearing. Watt watched the surrounding trees for any sign of trouble.

Susan didn't want to look, but she couldn't do anything else. Jason lay still. *He's so pale.* She flopped onto the grass beside her cousin.

What could she do? She gulped back tears. *This is my fault,* she thought.

Katerina stepped hesitantly from behind a tree.

"At last you've come," she murmured. "I have waited so long. We have to leave here now."

"What happened here?" Watt asked her.

"We have to leave, I said." Katerina drew herself up. "I have to get to Cologne."

"What happened here?" Watt asked again.

Katerina's shoulders slumped. She sat heavily across from Susan. They looked at each other over Jason's prone form.

"He saved me," she started. "He was so brave." She sniffed.

Susan thought back to the Jason she knew. Sick, in pain, but never complaining. Always thinking of others. And then here in the Holy Roman Empire. Adventuring.

"Stalwart," she murmured to herself.

Katerina nodded. "Yes, stalwart."

Watt sighed. "What happened here?" He still stood, his eyes roving over the forest, his knife at the ready.

Katerina looked up. "Men came. I was teaching Jason the names of some of the things around here." She turned to Susan. "He doesn't speak our language, you know. Not even Latin."

Watt sighed. "What happened here, my lady?"

"Oh, yes, men came. They said that they noticed my fine dress and shoes, and they thought there would be some other fine things in my bag. They passed us this morning when we were walking with the children." She looked up at Watt. "I told you I'd be recognized."

Watt looked concerned. He shifted his feet. "Did they know who you were or just that you were richer than the other children?"

"Jason didn't give them time to tell a big story. When they rushed up, the two of them grabbed me straight away. One—the really smelly one—had a knife, and he waved it in my face. The other piggy one grabbed at my bag. He pulled. I pulled. He was yelling for the other one to use his knife to cut the straps on the bag. That's when Jason hit him across the knees with a tree branch. That one screamed and fell over backward. But he still had hold of my bag, and so I fell on top of him. Ugh. The pig with the knife jumped over us on the ground and ran at Jason, but he brandished his branch in both hands and hit the pig upside the head. He had a battle cry. Base-baseball, he yelled. But he didn't have a ball at all. Just the branch. So that meant the two attackers were on the ground. I still had hold of my bag, but Smelly was a lot bigger and stronger than me so he tipped me over and wrenched the bag from my hands. But Sir Jason—he is my knight—gave his battle cry again. Baseball. He used his branch when the man got up to run with the bag. He hit Smelly right here." Katerina pointed at a spot just by her ear." I took my bag back and stood out of the way.

"Smelly groaned and held up his hands. Sir Jason had the branch held over his shoulder, and he scowled at the man. He made just one threatening move toward Smelly, and he started babbling about the mistake they'd made and how they'd just hurry along now. Smelly helped Piggy to his feet, and they both limped away. Jason followed them as they hobbled off. The one with the sore legs was sniveling about telling the mayor about us. They had a cart back in the woods. Just a small one with a donkey.

Sir Jason made them leave it, and they went off along the road."

"What if they come back?" Katerina flapped her hands. "What will I do?" Katerina sank into silence, her story told.

Watt and Susan exchanged glances. What next?

Susan looked down at Jason. So pale and still.

"But if all that happened and Jason—Sir Jason—drove off the bad guys, why is he laid out like this?"

"Ah." Katerina nodded. "I don't know what happened. He walked back into the clearing. Asked me if I was all right—most courteously—and then his eyes rolled up into his head, and he just crumpled to the ground. It was awful. He fell all crumpled, but I laid him straight and folded his hands, as is proper. I can see no wounds, but something has laid him low. Gone so quickly." She shook her head sadly.

Susan looked over at her cousin. So quickly. She wanted to just reach into her pocket and pull out the crystal. She wanted out of this situation. She didn't even like this stuck-up girl, and now Jason was dead because he helped her. Was helping Katerina get to Cologne so important that it was worth Jason dying?

She sneaked her hand into her pocket. If she held Jason tight, could she take him back with her? She reached out her hand. Gently she stroked his cheek.

He was warm.

"Dead people are supposed to be cold, aren't they?"

Both Watt and Katerina nodded. Watt crouched down and held the blade of his knife under Jason's nose. It fogged.

Watt leaped to his feet. "He lives," he shouted.

Susan had no words for the feelings that rushed through her. She felt pulled in so many directions. Relief, happiness, uncertainty, guilt. She shook her shoulders. She had no time for that.

Susan reached forward and gently slapped his face. "Jason," she called. "Jason, can you hear me?"

Nothing.

"Jason. I need you to come here now."

Nothing.

"Come on. You've laid around long enough."

Nothing.

I hope he's not in a coma.

She gave his face a hard slap.

Jason took a deep breath and blew it out. "I'm soooo hungry," he moaned.

Susan burst into tears of relief. She put her head down on his chest and sobbed. She felt a pat on her shoulder and looked up. She met Jason's eyes.

"I'm really hungry, really," he said.

Of course.

Watt dropped the food bag at her feet. Her fingers fumbled the knots in her hurry.

What did they have that she could feed him quickly? She spread out the food they had. Something quick and easy. Something they didn't have to cook. The honey. Yes. That was supposed to be good for you.

Her fingers fumbled with the stopper in the top of the pot.

Watt gently took it from her and pulled the cork with his teeth. He smiled as he passed the little pot back to her.

Susan poured the honey into Jason's mouth. He swallowed. "So sweet," he said, but he gulped another mouthful.

Jason struggled to sit up.

Katerina held out a chunk of bread, and Susan poured the honey onto it. Jason ate it eagerly.

"Oh, Sir Jason, you are my knight. Thank you." Katerina looked over her shoulder. "They will come back and bring others. We must move. We must hide. Now."

"Right." Jason tried to stand but slumped back onto the ground. Susan handed him a plum.

An awful braying sound split the quiet. Katerina and Susan both sprang to their feet and stood together, covering the position where Jason lay.

Watt walked into the clearing, leading the villains' donkey with the little cart trailing behind. He shrugged. "It's not a carriage. But we have to move."

While Watt helped Jason stand and climb into the cart, Katerina stood by, watching anxiously. Jason had to crumple up to fit. The edge of the cart dug into his back.

"Use this as padding." She threw her bag into the cart.

"But we'll be seen on the road. They have seen us all together, and they know that we are traveling toward Cologne."

Susan smiled at Katerina. "Ah, no, you and I are going to disappear."

Katerina pulled away. "Not witchcraft."

Susan shook her head. "Nothing like that. Just a little trick I learned on a ship once."

Susan drew Katerina into the trees.

CHAPTER 15
DISGUISED

Susan expected an argument from Katerina about disguising herself as a boy. After all, Watt had suggested that Katerina was a lady and would be mortified to appear in boy's clothing. She would be disgracing her family by donning the pants and tunic they had bought for her.

Susan carefully opened the bundle of clothing in front of Katerina.

Katerina snatched up the pants and shook them out. She held them up. "Good idea," she said. "I hope they will be of a size for me." She looked back at the bundle. "What tunic did you acquire?"

Astounded and pleased, Susan handed over the rest of the outfit.

Katerina turned her back to Susan so she could undo the lacings holding Katerina's dress on.

"I'm surprised," Susan said as she struggled to get the knot untied. "Watt thought you would object to disguising yourself as a boy."

Katerina laughed. "Watt only knows the public me. Frederic and I always used to slip out of the castle into the town when we were children. It never would have worked if we had been dressed in our usual clothes."

Susan finally had the knot undone and started loosening the back all the way up.

"The first time we tried it," Katerina went on, "I used one of my maid's dresses, and we were spotted." She chuckled again. "We hadn't been in the streets for more than a few minutes when Grandmama Beatrice pulled up in her carriage, and we were dragged back to the palace.

"Aaah," Katerina sighed as Susan finally had all the laces undone.

Quickly they lifted the heavy dress over Katerina's head.

"So then, after that, Frederick acquired some old clothing from one of the grooms, and we hid it in the orchard. As boys we found we could get in and out and go around the town without being recognized. It was a lot of fun."

Quickly Katerina climbed into the pants and tunic. She twirled around. "What do you think?"

Susan took a long look. "Good, good," she said. "But make your movements more boyish, I think. Boys don't usually twirl around like that."

Katerina nodded and put her hands on her hips with her feet wide apart. "More like this?" She grinned.

Susan laughed. "That's more like it. Boys do like to strut."

"What about you, though?" Katerina asked. "It would be better if you were a boy, too. If we are all boys we can travel more easily. People won't question four lads traveling together, but three lads and a girl will raise eyebrows. People will notice and remember."

"I've played a boy before." Susan fumbled with the bow on her skirt. "I learned to blend in with a group of boys once, so it won't be hard for me to do it again." She grabbed the ties and unwound her wraparound skirt. Under it she wore a pair of jeans pulled up to her knees.

Katerina watched as Susan rolled down the pants. "They're like Jason's," she observed.

Susan settled the jeans on her waist. "I left home in a big hurry, and I wanted to have the skirt on, so I put it over what I was already wearing."

"Ladies wear pants like those where you live?" Katerina sounded shocked.

"Yes, everyone does." Susan folded her skirt. *I better not tell her about shorts.*

To change the subject, Susan gestured through the trees. "Shall we join the *other* boys?"

The two strutted out to where Watt and Jason waited with the cart.

Watt looked up, surprised. He walked around the two. Jason chuckled from the cart.

"I dub you Serge and George," he said.

"Works for me." Susan nodded. "Come on, George. We need to get on the road."

Watt whacked the donkey on its rump and the four "boys" set off on the road to Cologne.

"I'm still hungry, though," Jason said.

"Have a plum," Susan offered.

CHAPTER 16
KATERINA'S STORY

Over the next hour, Susan learned that a little donkey could only go so fast, no matter how hard you push it. And she could only go so fast, too. Footsore and panting, she needed a rest.

The others looked just as tired. Except for Jason. He was comfy in the cart and eating his way steadily through the food bought at the market.

"We need horses," Watt groaned. "We can't keep this up all the way to Cologne. We're only just coming level with the town again, and market day is almost over."

Katerina nodded. "Yes, horses." She fished in her bag. "We have the money. Get horses, Watt." She leaned against the cart and eased her feet. "Now that I am George, we can have horses."

Watt took the money and headed into the town again.

Katerina watched him go. "He is a good judge of horseflesh."

Together they pulled the donkey and cart off the road and into the forest. Susan unhitched the donkey, and the cart slumped forward, tipping Jason out onto the grass.

Gingerly, he climbed to his feet and stretched. "I feel much better," he said. He turned to Susan. "I've been thinking about it. I realized that I've been silly. I arrived here feeling so great and pain free that I forgot that I still had a weak body. And then we walked and ran and fought and didn't get much to eat, so it's no wonder that I collapsed."

Susan nodded. "Talk about burning the candle at both ends. It's a wonder you kept going at all."

"What about candles?" Katerina butted in. "You're talking about candles. Do you have candles?"

They both turned to Katerina. "Sorry. We left you out of the conversation." Susan apologized, and Jason bowed gallantly to her.

The donkey quietly began grazing on the grass nearby, and the trio slumped thankfully against a mossy log to rest. Jason shared out the last of the grapes.

"Now would be a good time for you to explain what the problem is," Susan pointed out to Katerina.

"We are helping you and still don't understand why you are running away to Cologne."

Katerina sighed. "It is a long story and so complicated."

Jason scooted along the log until his shoulder was touching Susan's.

Susan nodded to Katerina. "Well, it seems we have time, so why don't you begin?"

Katerina leaned back against the log, crossed her feet at the ankles, and nodded.

"My family is the Hohenstaufen," she began. "Sir Gustaff and his family are Welfs. I was sent by my grandmother to be fostered among them as a sort of friendly gesture of trust."

Susan couldn't help it. She had to butt in. "Bully Gustaff didn't seem too friendly to me."

Katerina continued. "Noble children are always sent to live elsewhere as they grow up. It is our way. Watt was sent by his family to my cousin Frederick so he could grow up knowing all the people there. It was a great honor for Watt to be accepted into Frederick's court."

"Was it an honor for you to go to the Welf court?"

Katerina shook her head. "They should have been honored to have me there." She closed her fist. "They're oafs."

Katerina sat up and began pulling tufts of grass. "I arrived there in the summer of the year of our Lord

1211. Their cousin Otto was the emperor at the time, and the Welfs were proud and arrogant. It would have been advantageous for me to form a match with one of the Welfs, but none of them were to my liking.

"But Emperor Otto IV was allied with King John of England. He is his nephew and grew up in the English court. King John sent an envoy to the court of Gustaff's father."

"Sir Robert," Susan guessed.

Katerina smiled and nodded. "Yes. He was appalled at the rowdy ways of the Welf court, so we naturally spent more and more time together. He is a fine singer and nimble fingered on the lute.

"For me, it was an ideal alliance. If I married Sir Robert, I would eventually travel to England, far away from the political fighting between the Welfs and the Hohenstaufen."

Katerina shook her head and leaned forward. "Then everything changed. Otto IV got greedy. Even though he was emperor of the Holy Roman Empire, he wanted all of Italy as well. He made plans. He called for knights and soldiers. The lesser dukes and princelings were not happy. They needed peace, not war. They regretted electing him emperor over Frederick the Hohenstaufen, who should have rightfully become the emperor.

"So, as the leaves fell in the beech forests last year, they all got together and voted Otto out and

Frederick in as emperor. You can imagine that Otto was outraged, and so he immediately declared war on Frederick, king of Sicily."

Susan sat forward, too. "This cousin Frederick you talk about. He's the emperor?"

Katerina nodded. "He will be once he's crowned."

"That must have been hard for you, stuck in the middle of the Welf family," Jason spoke up.

Katerina rubbed her hands together.

"When the news arrived, I went from being a guest to being a hostage in the blink of an eye." She continued on. "My grandmother sent a party of soldiers to bring me home, but they were sent away very rudely.

"In the spring of this year, Pope Innocent III, declared Frederick emperor of the Holy Roman Empire. And so Frederick began gathering his allies and moving his army into position to take back his lands.

"That's when Frederick sent Watt to sneak into the castle and try to find a way to free me—quietly. He thought that where a troop of soldiers sent to fetch me had failed, one brave person of about my own age might be able to subtly sneak me away. Watt began working in the stables.

"I wasn't in all that much of a hurry to go. The road was dangerous. I was sick of all the pushing and pulling of politics that had gone on. Sir Robert was still there, and he and I were going to be betrothed. But then something else happened that made it really urgent that I get away and back to my grandmother in Cologne."

Jason and Susan both leaned forward even farther. "What?" Susan murmured.

Katerina nodded once. "Frederick was in Genoa, building support among the nobles there, and Otto was moving into position to oppose him. One day, I was sitting in my usual spot in the gardens. I was reading, and I liked to tuck myself into the bower so that the big red roses draped all around me. It smelled a lot better than the rest of the castle. It was a wonderful spot to be quiet and where I could find some peace. But this day it wasn't peace I found. It was a conspiracy.

"Gustaff and his father entered the garden, and as I didn't want to speak with them, I drew even farther back into the roses. They sat on the bench beside the path. I heard every horrible word they said.

"A messenger had been captured. Frederick had sent the man with a message for the French king, Philip Augustus. Frederick wanted to arrange a meeting with the French king or his son, Prince Louis, at Vaucouleurs in the autumn. He wanted to assure the French that he was their ally and that Otto was the enemy. The Welfs had slain the messenger but kept the written message.

"Gustaff's father planned to send another messenger to the French with the message. He wanted the meeting to take place, or really, he wanted Frederick to travel to the meeting.

"While I listened, the two of them plotted how they would have an assassin waiting along the route. Frederick would be murdered in his bed, and that would be the end of it. They laughed as they talked about it. The cowards. No knightly battle for them, just a cowardly knife in the dark. It was hard to stay hidden while they chatted on, sitting at their ease in the sunshine, as though all the world was going in their direction.

"I had to get away to warn Frederick. I couldn't send a message. There was no one I could trust with this information. I was concerned that if Watt brought the news to Frederick, he would not be believed. It was knowledge too dangerous to put to paper. I had to get away.

"Watt and I worked to find a solution. I had to slip away and get to Cologne to the protection of my grandmother's house, and then the full might of the Hohenstaufen family would come into play. We thought of just riding out on the best horses in the stables, but we knew we would be overtaken.

"And then, like an answer from God, all these children began flocking through the town. They came to the castle, looking for food, and the kitchens gave them supplies. Watt and I realized that we could use the children as cover and slip away among them. Nobody would think of looking for a Hohenstaufen among a lowly gaggle of peasant children—and they were heading for Cologne.

"So we slipped away and joined the throng of children. We didn't realize that they would be so slow." Katerina shrugged. "You know the rest."

Susan let out a long breath she hadn't realized she'd been holding.

"Now I understand why you have to hurry to Cologne," she said. "You were lucky that the children came along when they did."

Katerina nodded. "Yes, we were lucky. But Sir Gustaff still came along. He would have beaten all those children. He would have killed Grefin to be sure I wasn't with them. You came out of nowhere and solved that situation. So, yes, we were lucky."

Katerina stood. She automatically moved her hands to smooth down her skirts and then shook them as she realized there was no skirt to settle. She turned her head as though listening.

Susan heard it, too. The sound of horses approaching. Both she and Jason stood. Ready. Were the approaching horses with Watt, or was it another band of searchers riding toward Cologne?

CHAPTER 17
HORSES

The three drew farther back into the trees. The horses slowed. Susan could clearly hear the rhythm of the hooves change. Gallop, canter, trot, walk. A group of horses were now walking toward them. The three held their breath. The horses stopped.

"I heard there were three boys hanging around here. I think they're the ones we're looking for." They heard a gruff, raspy voice.

Katerina sighed. "Waa-aat," she exclaimed and stepped out into the open.

"Not funny," Susan added as she joined her.

Jason shrugged as he stepped up to the closest horse. "I thought it was almost funny," he said as he stroked the horse's nose.

Susan eyed the horses. They were standing still, blowing a little from their run. One stamped its hoof on the ground and pulled on the lead to move closer to the grass beside the road. The saddles were very different from any she had ever seen. They looked like little arm chairs perched on top of the horse.

Susan took a step back. "Um," she began. "Which do you think is the quietest horse?" Three sets of eyes turned to her.

"You can't ride?" Jason asked. He walked over to her and put his hand on her shoulder. His horse followed along.

"We walked Blaze around the paddock once," Susan said, straightening her tunic and adjusting her hat. "How come you're so confident around that horse?"

Jason smiled and stroked the horse's neck. "For Christmas one year, I got a fortnight at a riding camp."

"You learned to ride in the snow?"

Jason laughed. He poked his finger at his chest. "Australia," was all he said.

Watt led a horse over to Susan. He put the reins into one hand and slipped an apple into the other.

Susan looked up, puzzled.

"Put the apple on your hand and feed it to the horse," Watt advised.

And so Susan did. The horse approached even closer. It reached out its head and snuffled at her hand. Susan took a deep breath and watched closely. She was ready to snatch her hand back, but she held steady. The horse had lips, she noticed. Lips that reached out and pulled the apple into its mouth. The horse munched contentedly. Susan reached out her hand and gently stroked the horse's nose. The horse munched on. Susan breathed in the horsy smell. Hay and sweat and a hint of leather. Keeping hold of the reins, Susan moved to the side of the horse and began stroking its neck. It was warm and slightly damp under her hand.

All of a sudden, a word popped into her head. Out of nowhere. "I'll call you Myrtle," she said.

"Myrtle." Jason laughed. "It's a horse, not a ghost." Then he added, "Mount up, cowboy. We need to ride."

CHAPTER 18

TO COLOGNE

And ride they did.

Watt and Jason rode their horses close in on either side of Susan to lend her support until she got the hang of it.

"Don't push your foot so far into the stirrups."

"Keep the reins firm."

"Don't lift your arms up."

"Try not to bounce so much."

Susan's head rang with all the advice they tossed at her.

The only way I'm going to get them to shut up is to figure this out, she decided. And so she concentrated and let her body feel its way into the rhythm of the horse. Myrtle. Susan grinned to herself and leaned forward to pat Myrtle's neck.

They stopped briefly in the market square of the town. Susan was glad to dismount. *Ow, I'm going to ache tonight.* Her saddle rubbed her in places that made walking painful. She limped around in a small circle, trying to get the kinks out of her legs.

Jason dismounted easily. He patted down the horse's neck and gently walked it in a circle. He looked over at Susan with a smile. He shook his head and tutted away. "Myrtle." He chuckled.

Susan limped over to stand beside him. "Well, what did you call yours?" She poked her chin toward Jason's horse.

"He's Bunyip," Jason replied, patting his horse's neck.

"Huh?"

"It's a proud Australian name for a fierce and scary beast."

Susan shrugged. "OK. If you say so." She stroked Bunyip gently.

Myrtle snorted and blew on her neck. Susan laughed and turned to her horse. "OK, you get a pat, too."

"You will quickly become a fine horsewoman, I can see." Katerina strode up to where Susan and Jason were standing with the horses. She was juggling fruit and vegetables in her arms and wore a large, floppy hat. "Watt said you had a way of making a bag to carry all this food," she added.

Susan laughed and dug out her cloth again. "Yep, I can do that," she said and spread the cloth along a bench.

As soon as Katerina was free of her burden, she took back the reins of her horse. "Watt is bargaining for another bag," she said. "He has food, too. We want to give some to Grefin and the children if we pass them along the way."

"Good idea." Jason nodded. "They helped us, and they need all the help they can get."

Watt soon returned. Quickly they mounted up and rode quietly out of town on the road to Cologne.

Once they were through the houses and back out into the countryside, they set the horses for a gallop. They were on their way.

⊨⊣ ⊢⊨

Gradually, the flow of people drifting home from the market dwindled away, but the road was still busy with children. So many children on the road, and all heading for Cologne.

Susan could only stare as they walked their horses through the throngs of pilgrims that clogged the road. Children of all ages moved along. Mostly footsore and weary, they slowly trod the path, but all had their heads firmly turned toward Cologne. When the road they were traveling met with other paths, more children moved onto the main road. The groups mixed and mingled.

They all watched for any sign of Grefin and the children they had traveled with, and eventually the sound of Petriona's cough allowed them to recognize their group.

Katerina slowed her horse and turned in her saddle to untie the bag of food behind her.

"Wait," Susan called. "We don't want them to know what we look like now."

Katerina looked around. "I can't just throw the food at them as we canter by," she said with a scowl.

They pulled their horses to the side.

"True." Susan nodded. "But we can't let them see us." Susan waved her hand around their little group. "We're not us anymore."

Quickly they settled on a plan. They waited and watched the children passing them by until they spied a small group of children led by a responsible-looking boy and girl. Watt jumped down from his horse and walked out into the road.

The little group stopped. The smaller children huddled behind the two leaders.

"We are peaceful pilgrims," the boy said, holding out his hands to show that he carried no weapon.

Watt matched the gesture. "Blessed be," he said.

Then Watt put his arm around the shoulders of the boy and explained that he had two bags of food and that he wanted it delivered to a certain group of pilgrims who were just ahead.

"Food?" The boy looked with interest at the bags.

"It would serve you well to join your group with Grefin's group," Watt suggested. "There is food enough in these bags to see you all to Cologne. We owe Grefin a debt of gratitude, and we want to ensure that he receives this food for his children—and for yours."

The boy nodded. "The Lord has provided. It will be as you wish. How will we know this Grefin?"

Watt described the group and Grefin in particular. The boy took one of the bags and the girl the other. They slung them over their shoulders and set off along the road, followed by their little gaggle of children. There seemed to be a new lightness in their steps.

It had been a long day for everyone. The sun was low in the sky, and the pilgrims were moving into the fields along the side of the road. It was time to camp for the night. Susan spotted Grefin's group. They were gathering wood to start a fire.

The four "lads" kept their heads well down, and with the road clear again, they cantered on.

The cool of the evening slid over them. Watt and Jason still rode close on either side of Susan. Mostly she had Myrtle under control, but she felt safer with their support. Now Katerina led.

Jason groaned.

"Are you hurt?" Susan looked over to see if she could see any blood.

"We gave away all the food. I'm so hungry."

Now that Jason had drawn her attention to the fact, Susan realized that she hadn't eaten much all day. She was hungry, but she worried about Jason. Remembering how sickly he had been before they arrived in this time and all the things he had done since they arrived, she felt that he must be draining any reserves of energy his body possessed.

"I'm hungry, too," she agreed.

Watt nodded to them and rode forward to keep pace beside Katerina.

Susan could see them talking but could not hear what they said over the clatter of their horses' hooves. It was obvious to her that Watt was suggesting that they find some food. Katerina just wanted to ride on into the night. Watt pointed to the horses several times. He pointed emphatically to Katerina and then to Susan and Jason.

Eventually Susan saw Katerina nod reluctantly. Watt reined in his horse and then fell into step beside them again.

"We're stopping at the next hostelry we find," he said. "Katerina agrees that the horses need to be rested and fed," he added sarcastically.

Susan and Jason nodded in relief. Susan would be so glad to get off Myrtle for a while.

CHAPTER 19
THE HOSTELRY

Just as the sun dipped below the trees and evening dark crept in, they rounded a corner and saw an inn in front of them.

Susan heaved a sigh of relief, and that brought with it the wonderful odor of stew. She sniffed the air. Chicken stew. Susan gave Myrtle a nudge in the ribs and set off at a trot for the stables she could see on one side.

By the time the others clattered up behind her, she was already pulling her bag from Myrtle's back. Her legs cramped as soon as she tried to take a step. *I need to do some serious stretching*, she realized, gripping her saddle for support.

The stable doors opened and hostlers hurried into the yard to take the horses.

Jason threw his arms around the shoulders of Susan and Katerina. "Serge," he whispered and squeezed Katerina's shoulder. "George," he added and gave Susan a little shake.

Both girls nodded quietly; it was easy to forget. Susan shook herself, threw her bag over her shoulder, and tried to swagger toward the glowing doorway. The others caught up with her and laughing, they entered the inn arm in arm.

Noise. Clamor. They entered a crowded room. The smell of the chicken stew was now coupled with the smell of too many people, spilled beer, and smoke. The room was dimly lit by candles in sconces on the walls and on the tables. Watt led the way through the crowd and found them a place on the end of a long wooden table. They sat on wooden benches. *Like a picnic table,* Susan thought.

Jason leaned over and whispered in Susan's ear, "Not the Ritz."

Susan nodded. "That's for sure." Then she added, "I'm so hungry I don't care."

Jason smiled. "Now you sound like me."

A young girl bustled up to them. She was lugging a huge tray laden with tankards. Beer slopped out onto the floor as she turned to look at them. "What do you want?"

Watt told her to bring some of the stew for each of them and some watered wine.

"Show us yer money," the girl ordered.

Watt plonked a few coins on the table. The girl nodded and strode away to deliver her tray of beer.

Katerina leaned toward Watt. "Surely there is a quiet room we can rent so we can have some privacy and comfort."

Watt shook his head. "No, George, we eat here if we don't want to draw attention to ourselves. Four boys getting a private room to eat in would be noticed by all." He shook his head again. "That's what privileged nobles do."

The girl returned, slapped down four meals and four mugs of...something...and turned to scurry away. Watt grabbed her skirt. "We need beds for later," he told her.

She nodded once and pulled away from Watt's hand.

"Serge and I want you to get two rooms, not just beds," Katerina informed him.

Watt sighed. "Yes, my...George, I'll see what I can do."

Susan turned her attention to the meal in front of her. It smelled so good but looked strange. There was no plate. The stew was dumped into/onto a small loaf of bread. All the juices had soaked into the bread. Susan could see gobs of meat. Watt and Katerina produced spoons from somewhere and began to eat quickly.

Susan looked around. Where was the cutlery? The people on the other tables had spoons and ate hungrily. "Ah." She remembered and fished around in her bag and came up with a spoon. "I wondered why Mrs. Coleman had a spoon in there," she said to Jason.

"Is there two?" Jason asked with a woebegone look.

Susan shook her head. "I'll eat fast." And she did. Once she had eaten all the meat and vegetables, she saw that the juices had soaked into the bread, making that tasty, too, so she handed the spoon to Jason and picked up the bread in her hands.

"Delicious." Susan sighed with satisfaction when she dropped the last crust onto the table.

Katerina shrugged. "Anything tastes good, Serge, when you're really hungry."

Susan lifted her mug. She was thirsty. She twirled the cup, and wrinkled her nose at the sharp smell. *Yuk, vinegary.* She took a small sip. *Vinegar mixed with muddy water.* She spat it out. "That is truly awful." She spluttered and thumped the mug on the table. She swiped at her eyes which were watering.

Katerina sipped and agreed. "You can't expect decent wine in a place like this."

"Water then. I need something to drink."

"I'll go." Watt stood. "I have to arrange for rooms anyway."

"Thank you." Susan stretched. "It will be good to get a good night's sleep."

Watt bowed slightly to her. "Cologne tomorrow," he said with a smile.

CHAPTER 20
THE STABLE

Jason ate every bite of his meal. Even the last nub of crust went into his mouth. He stretched with a satisfied sigh and hooked one leg over the corner of the table.

"That's better," he said and burped loudly.

His manners didn't faze Katerina. She hooked her leg over the other corner of the table, and the two of them fell to a game they played together. Katerina told Jason the name of something, and he repeated it. On and on. Jason was learning.

Susan scooped up her spoon and thrust it into her bag. "I think I'll go out and check on the horses," she said. Jason waved to her, deep in the game. She limped through the crowd toward the door.

She met Watt on the way.

"I have just one room for us," he said. "But it has four beds, so that's good."

Susan nodded. The thought of a bed sounded wonderful. "I'm just going to check on the horses," she said. "I'll be up soon."

Watt removed his neckerchief. "I'll leave this tied around the latch for you." He moved on to fetch the others.

Stepping out into the night air was like entering a new world. After the smoke and fug of the inn, Susan stood for a moment and took deep breaths of the fresh air. After the second breath, she could feel the freshness all the way to the bottom of her lungs. She stretched her arms out wide to take in the night.

From the doorway, she located the stable. Dim light seeped out under the doorway. Susan stopped in the shadows and gently began some stretches. The ride had seized up her shoulder muscles as well as her legs, she discovered. It felt good to get the kinks out. Once she felt limber again, she wandered across the yard and gently pushed on the stable door. It opened with a creak. The smell of hay and oats and horses met her. Horse stalls lined both walls of the long, narrow space. Susan walked along the lines, looking for Myrtle. She passed a small room off to the side and could see two boys sitting inside. One jumped to his feet as Susan appeared in the doorway.

"Can we help you sir?" He bobbed his head.

Susan waved her arm toward the horse stalls and shook her head with a smile.

She ambled on down the line.

A snort attracted her attention to the right, and there was Myrtle with her head poking over the top of the stall. Susan felt like she had found a friend. She hurried across to Myrtle's stall. Right by the door, but out of Myrtle's reach, stood a basket of apples. Susan grabbed one and held it out to her horse just as Watt had shown her.

Myrtle snuffled it up and looked around for another one. With a chuckle Susan let herself into the stall and patted and stroked Myrtle's flank. The horse was warm and strong and solid. Susan let out a sigh and sank down to sit in the hay. To her surprise, Myrtle sank down, too. Susan rested her head on Myrtle's side. She felt warm and comfortable.

Except that something was digging into her thigh. She reached into her pocket and pulled out her crystal. She was surprised. *I haven't thought about the crystal, moving in time, or home since this morning,* she realized. The thought brought a smile to her face. *This adventure is so different.* Even though the stable was only dimly lit, the crystal sparkled in her hand. Those sparkles made it seem like the crystal was saying, "I'm here. You're doing great."

Now in the quiet of the stable with only Myrtle for company, Susan took stock of all that had happened in the last couple of days.

Jason was so different. He was full of adventure and knew a lot of stuff about survival. He made a great traveling companion. Susan liked his company. She worried, though. He was so deathly ill in their own time, and although he seemed fine here, he had fainted. She wondered if she should use the crystal to try to take him home—to sickness and a dull life of sitting around. If she did take him home, would he be healthy like now or sick as he had been? What a question. Susan knew that Jason didn't want to leave this time. He was enjoying the adventure, but Susan wanted to keep him safe. Jason was important to her, but her crystal responsibility was to help Katerina get to her grandmother.

Katerina. What a surprise she was. At first Katerina had seemed so snobby, but then, once you got to know her, she was really brave. And loyal, too. She was in all this danger mainly to get a warning to her cousin. And fancy having a cousin who was an emperor. Now that was something. Susan felt that it was right for Jason and herself to be helping Katerina and Watt to save the emperor. Frederick—that was his name. And tomorrow they would be in Cologne and Katerina could contact her grandmother and that would be that. Mission accomplished.

But that left Grefin and the straggly children who were planning to walk to Jerusalem. Susan shook her head. It was not right. It was dangerous. She could admire their passion and faith, but they were dreadfully ill-equipped to accomplish what they expected. They didn't understand how far away Jerusalem was. She would have liked to help them, but she didn't know how. They had so little.

Susan sighed and bumped her head against Myrtle's flank. Myrtle snorted as if she understood what Susan was thinking. It was quiet and warm in the stable. She could hear the quiet conversation of the two stableboys softly in the background. Occasionally a horse snorted or stamped a hoof, but the overall feeling was of rest and quiet. *I should just sleep here,* Susan thought. *Nope, Jason will worry about where I am.* Susan climbed to her feet and gave a lovely stretch. It felt so good to push her arms out and then to flex her knees.

Susan reached for the latch on the stall door. *Bam. Bang.* Clatter of hooves. Men yelling and stamping. Susan quickly ducked down into the stall again.

"Get out here, boy," one of the men yelled.

A fist thumped into the wall.

"Now, boy. We've got horses. Get out here."

Susan shrank farther into the shadows of the stall. She knew that voice. Sir Gustaff had arrived.

All was a flurry of sound.

Susan had to warn the others. How could she? Right now she was so scared she didn't think she could make her legs move.

So far all the noise and activity was centered around the doors. Susan peered cautiously over the wall of the stall. Horses were being unsaddled, and the men accompanying Sir Gustaff were taking traveling packs from the backs of a couple of spare horses. Soon they would be moving into the front room of the inn.

I hope the others have gone up to bed.

Sir Gustaff leaned against the wall, watching everything progress. One of the stableboys was tending to Sir Gustaff's horse. As he removed the saddle, the buckle from the girth strap slapped back onto the horse's flank. The horse whinnied in pain and sashayed sideways. Sir Gustaff lurched from the wall and backhanded the lad across the head.

"Watch what you're doing, oaf." Gustaff scowled down at the boy who was lying flat in the straw.

The boy sprang to his feet and gestured at the horse. "Look at his flank," he said. "Just look. The girth has been pulled too tight and left too long. There are sores under the strap." The boy put his hands on his hips and glared at Sir Gustaff.

Susan gulped.

Gustaff loomed over the boy. "Are you saying that I don't look after my horse?" He sneered down at the boy.

The boy ducked his head. "I'll put some salve on it," he said quietly.

The boy turned and, taking the horse's reins, led the horse along the row until he came to the stall where Susan was hiding. He hesitated for a moment, and then he opened the door to the next stall and ushered the horse inside. All the time he was making kind, soothing noises to the horse.

He knows I'm here.

Thump. The wall between the stalls shuddered. *The horse,* Susan thought. *No, wait. Horses' hooves make a sharper sound than that. The boy kicked the wall.* Susan crept across the straw and lightly tapped on the wall. There was an answering tap.

The boy came out of the stall and leaned a huge bale of hay on the front wall of her stall. He looked out around it and winked at her. Then he jerked his head. *He wants me to follow him.*

Susan cautiously left the stall. She took the front side of the bale and the two of them moved off toward the back of the stable. The boy walked to make it look as though he was carrying the entire load.

They guided the huge bale into the last door on the right and dropped it with a sigh of relief. Susan looked around. They were in a small room stacked with spare saddles and brushes and other horsy stuff. There were also jars and boxes that probably contained salves and ointments to help injured horses—or stableboys. The boy put his fingers to his lips and moved to the back of the room.

He opened a small door in the wall and gestured for Susan to slip through. He smiled, but Susan saw him wince. His face was swelling from the blow Sir Gustaff had given him.

Susan hurried to the door. "What is your name?" she asked.

"I'm Eric," he said and bobbed his head.

"Thank you," she whispered as she scurried through the door and slid into the night. She heard the click as the door shut quietly behind her.

CHAPTER 21

SNEAKING IN

Susan pressed her back to the wall of the stable. She took a deep breath and let it out slowly. She squinted to peer through the darkness. Over in the courtyard, several torches burned. They made puddles of orange light on the cobblestones. Some light showed through the windows of the inn. There was one small light shining at the back of the inn.

As she watched, she saw some of the soldiers from Sir Gustaff's party making their way across the courtyard and in the front door. As they went, they yelled and jostled one another. They called for food and drink, lots of drink—very loudly.

Well, if that noise doesn't move Jason and the others out of the main room, I don't know what will, Susan thought. Hugging her bag close, she crept toward the back wall of the inn. She moved as quietly as she could. Fortunately, the landlord had made a path close to the wall, so it was almost easy going. When she came to the corner of the building she peeped around to make sure the coast was clear. A door banged open, and two men staggered out. They were leaning on each other, giggling and chortling in a slurred sort of way.

Susan watched them pass on their way to the privy. Quickly she moved to the door and opened it slowly. Light spilled into her face. Blinking, she took a quick peek and then shut the door again and drew back into the shadows. She wanted to process what she had seen in her quick glimpse. In front of her was a long, narrow passage that led into the main front room. Off to her right was an archway that seemed to lead to the kitchen. It was quite well lit, and she could hear sounds of pots and pans banging around. She hadn't seen the stairs to the upper level where she hoped her friends were sleeping.

She had to warn them. But first she had to be sure they weren't still in the taproom. *I'll just have to check it out*, she thought. *After all, I am a boy right now, and I have a right to be here. They won't recognize me.* She hoped.

Susan squared her shoulders and took another deep breath. She planted her feet wide apart and jammed her fists onto her hips. *Get that swagger going, Susan.*

She marched up to the door and swung it open so hard that it banged on the wall. *Oops, maybe not that much swagger.* She walked down the passageway, but as she drew level with the kitchen area, she couldn't resist peeping in. All was in turmoil. Cooks were wielding huge pans over an open fire. In one corner, a young girl was up to her elbows in suds. Dirty pots and pans were piled up all around her.

The serving girl from earlier brushed past Susan and rushed over to the table. "Hurry, hurry," she called. "These soldiers are not nice people. They want everything in a big hurry."

There were two trays of food sitting on the table, waiting to be taken out. The girl stooped wearily and grunted as she pulled one of the trays into her arms. *The perfect disguise.*

Susan hurried over and took the tray from the girl. "I'll help with that," she said. She staggered. The tray was so heavy. The girl sighed with relief. "Thank you, sir, that would be most helpful." She bobbed a curtsey and lifted the other tray.

Susan let the girl lead the way. They moved quickly down the passageway and out into the noise and clamor of the taproom. The girl rushed off to one side to deliver her tray of food. But Susan wanted to check out the room. So she moved to the table she had used earlier. She held the tray high so that her face was mostly covered. The table was occupied. Soldiers. That was good for the others. But not good for Susan.

"Set 'em down, lad, and hurry up about it." The soldier punched her in the arm to hurry her up. It hurt.

"Yes, sir," she gruffed and dumped the tray in the middle of the table. Hands grabbed at the trenchers, and Susan pulled the tray off the table again.

"Bring more beer," yelled the closest soldier.

"Plenty of it," added another.

"It's thirsty work hunting down runaways." A third laughed.

"And be quick." The closest one thumped her on the shoulder. Using the tray as a sort of shield, she hurried back through the room. She was relieved that her friends weren't in the taproom, but she still couldn't see the stairs to the sleeping rooms.

Susan intercepted the serving girl on her way back to the kitchen. She thrust the tray at her. "I delivered the meals to that table," she said. "How do I get to the sleeping rooms?"

The girl took the tray. "The stairs are through that door over there." She waved to the left and hurried on to the kitchen.

Susan slipped quickly through the door and shut it behind her. The door shut out the noise, and she took a moment to catch her breath before heading up the stairs.

Now, what was Watt going to leave on the latch so I would know which room?

CHAPTER 22

SNEAKING OUT

Susan opened the door to their room as quietly as she could. Four beds were crammed into the space. The ceiling sloped down to touch the floor in one corner. A small window occupied a tiny alcove in the roof line. Someone snored. All seemed asleep. One candle burned low on the bench by the one empty bed. The mattress looked thin and lumpy. The blanket looked stiff and scratchy. There were no sheets and no pillow that she could see. Susan sighed. It looked wonderful. If only she could lie down and shut her weary eyes and forget about the soldiers downstairs. And Sir Gustaff. Susan sighed again.

Watt was sleeping in the closest bed. She gently shook his shoulder. He started up with a gasp.

Before Susan knew what had happened, Watt was on his feet, knife in hand, crouched, ready to fight. He was still blinking sleep from his eyes.

"Shhhhhh." Susan put her fingers to her lips. "We need to be quiet." She pointed to indicate downstairs. "Gustaff and his men have arrived. They're everywhere."

Watt drew in a deep, calming breath. "You scared the life out of me," he said. He shook his head and grabbed for his belt, which was hanging at the end of his bed.

Susan nodded. "Scared is good." She moved to Jason's bed. He woke more calmly. Seeing Susan with her fingers pressed to her lips, he sat up quickly and threw back his blanket. "What's up?"

Katerina, disturbed by the rustling, sat up, too. "Susan, did you have to wake us all? Couldn't you have come in quietly?"

Susan shook her head. She sat down on her bed. The others gathered round, and she told them of the latest problem they had to face.

"But I didn't see Sir Gustaff in the taproom when I came through." She finished her tale.

Katerina nodded. "Oh yes, he would have demanded a private room for himself. He'll be tucked up somewhere."

Watt agreed.

"The soldiers downstairs told me they were looking for runaways."

Katerina sighed. "That's me, a runaway." Then she straightened her shoulders. "No I'm a Hohenstaufen, and I'm going to save my cousin so he can rule as emperor and sort out this mess that the Holy Roman Empire has become. No cowardly plot of the Welfs' can put our family down." By the end of that speech, Katerina was up and pacing between the beds.

"Well, we should leave while we can," Susan offered. "Most of them will be drunk or asleep. It will be harder to leave in the morning when they're all up and fresh."

"Maybe we could just hang out in the room until they're all gone and then take off," Jason suggested.

Watt shook his head. "Then they'll be between us and Cologne and we'll have to pass them to get into the city."

Silence fell. They all looked at their feet as though the solution to their problem lay on the floor.

"I know a back way into the stables," Susan said. "Eric let me out that way while Sir Gustaff was hanging around in the front."

Slowly and quietly, they gathered up the few possessions they had.

Watt opened the window. "We will have to go out this way," he said. "They've probably got a guard posted outside Gustaff's room."

Katerina peered out into the night. "Slate, not thatch," she muttered, relieved.

Susan stuck her head out into the darkness. She gulped. The roof wasn't too steep, but they were two stories high. Falling could break a leg. She remembered the stone path that bordered the walls. The tiles looked to be thin slabs of stone. She put out her hand. They felt cool and sturdy. Susan sniffed, there was smoke in the air from the chimneys. Yes, she could spot the kitchen fire. Best not to go there. Beyond that she could see the vast chimney for the fire in the common room. Too many people that way. To her right she could see another window sticking out into the roof line. No light showed. How could they reach the ground without a rope or something? And then there, she saw, just beyond the other window, a huge, spreading oak. Its branches stretched out over the roof and looked, to Susan, like an invitation. The leaves rustled in the slight breeze.

Cautiously they each climbed out onto the roof. Susan pulled off her runners and socks. Glad for the stretching she had done, she ventured onto the slates. They felt firm under her feet. Even though the tiles looked smooth, she could feel slight ridges in them. This helped her feet grip. Holding her arms wide for balance, she slid one foot slowly after the other and sidled toward the tree. Jason followed closely. Watt held Katerina's arm to steady her, but once she had her balance she shuffled along. Watt brought up the rear.

They needed to pass the other window, and Susan was soon there, listening at the sill. She heard snoring. Barely breathing, the four inched their way past and onto the tree.

The sturdy oak was a blessing. After the exposed roof, the tree gave shelter. The leaves enclosed them as they worked their way down from branch to branch. As they reached the path, each slipped into the bushes for cover. When all four were huddled together in the shelter of a rosemary hedge, they took a moment to relax.

It was only when the emergency was over and she was sprawled in the bushes that Susan realized how tense she had been on the roof. Once she had looked down, and for a moment if felt as though the ground was trying to suck her over the edge. *Now I know why they tell you not to look down when you're in high places.* She blew out a breath in relief.

"I'm glad I didn't have to do that in a dress," Katerina whispered with a grin.

Susan chuckled as she made her shoelaces double tight.

She stood and crooked her neck. The others stood, too, and they set off single file behind her. Susan wove her way through a vegetable garden toward the back of the stable.

They moved as quietly as they could. Every sound of their shoes on the path or rustle of their clothing seemed magnified about a million times. No moon shown. By starlight Susan could just see the dark outline of the stable. They crept along. Once Susan reached the stable wall, she moved her hand along, searching for the door latch.

The door creaked open a few inches. They started back against the wall. "Ssssh." Eric stood in the crack of the door. He motioned them forward. They slipped quietly into the stable.

As soon as they were inside with the door tightly shut behind them, Eric struck his flint and a candle shed a little light on the scene. All was quiet in the stalls. Somewhere a horse snorted and blew. That seemed to make the silence deeper. Eric motioned for them to follow him, and they did.

The three looked apprehensive. Was this a trap? Susan wasn't completely sure, but Eric had helped her before. *There comes a time when you just have to trust your instincts and go with what you feel,* she decided. She stepped out behind Eric and motioned for the others to follow, too. Watt slipped into an empty stall they passed, but Katerina and Jason followed along with her.

The front area of the stable was more brightly lit. Horse blankets had been rolled up and laid along the bottom of the door so that no light could seep out into the courtyard. The other stableboy stood there with a big grin on his face. At his feet lay one of Gustaff's men. He was unconscious and trussed up with what looked like reins.

"Left a guard, they did." The boy grinned. "Hopeless, he was." The boy pointed to himself with his thumb. "Peter, me," he said. "Belted him with a shovel, we did."

"Is he breathing?" Jason crept over to have a look.

Susan's attention, however, was caught by the sight of their horses. All four were saddled and ready to travel. Myrtle tossed her head and stamped her front hoof. She looked eager to run.

"They're ready for us." Susan looked with gratitude toward Eric. "How did you know?"

Eric shrugged. "Figured," was all he said.

Watt joined the group and tied his bag on behind his saddle.

The others moved toward their horses. But Eric stopped Susan with his hand.

"We need to be tied up, too," he said. "This guard didn't see who hit him. We made sure of that. But if we're not trussed up, too, they'll suspect us."

Watt came over to the group. "Of course," he said. "Sorry." He pulled his arm back to punch Eric in the face.

Susan grabbed his arm. "Not necessary," she said. "Look at the two of them. Eric and Peter have been beaten enough. We just need to tie them up."

Watt cracked his knuckles and grinned. "Yes, true," he said. "Get comfortable in the straw." He waved at the boys, inviting them to precede him into an empty stall.

The boys lay down with much chuckling, and Watt and Jason began tying them up with the reins they found hanging on hooks along the wall.

"We muffled the hooves for you," said Eric. "Take them off as soon as you're on your way."

Katerina knelt down between the two. She leaned forward and whispered something in their ears. Both smiled at her and nodded.

"Thank you." Susan came over and squatted down beside the boys. "Why are you helping us like this?"

Peter answered. "They're Welfs. You're not."

Watt blew out the candles so that the stable was in complete darkness. Susan and Jason opened the doors just enough for the horses to pass through and then pushed them shut behind them.

The four mounted up and walked their horses through the courtyard. The muffled hooves made little sound on the cobblestones. Just as they were about to ride under the arch leading to the road, Susan looked back at the inn. Standing in the window by the door was the shadowy figure of the serving girl she had helped. As Susan watched, she lifted her hand and waved a quiet farewell.

Susan turned in her saddle and got set for another painful day of learning how to ride.

CHAPTER 23
THE RIVER RHINE

At first they needed to proceed with care. No moon shone, so they had to rely on starlight to lead them.

All along the side of the road, they saw the embers of small fires. Pilgrim children, Susan supposed. All moving toward Cologne to hear the words of Nicholas. Ready to start their journey to Jerusalem. Susan sighed. The horses moved on into the night.

As the sky began to lighten, Susan became aware of the rush and gurgle of moving water. When she drew in a deep breath, she smelled mud. She sensed that a body of fresh water was close by. On her right, she could dimly see willow trees, their wispy fronds waving in the soft morning breeze. As it grew lighter still, she saw that little farms dotted the countryside to her left. As soon as she thought about it, she became aware of small farm sounds. Geese honked. Sheep bleated. Susan thought she heard a pig, too. A rooster crowed, and as if that were the signal, the sun peeped above the horizon, dazzling her.

Ahead of their small party, Susan saw the outline of a city. It was not a city of skyscrapers, but the daylight showed that they were approaching a large gathering of buildings. As the sun rose higher, it picked out the shape of a large church standing on a hill in the town.

"That's the cathedral we are building." Katerina stirred in her saddle. She stood in the stirrups and surveyed the city ahead with a broad smile. Watt, too, was smiling.

All along the road, people stirred. They stoked embers into bright fires. Blankets were shaken out. Children emerged from the trees to continue their plodding way into Cologne.

"Come on. Let's ride before the roads get clogged," Watt suggested with a wave of his hand.

Katerina hesitated. She ran her fingers through her unruly hair. She scratched. "I would like to clean up a little first," she said with a surprisingly shy smile.

Watt nodded once and turned his horse down a side path toward the water. They all followed in single file.

Susan brought up the rear, so she was the last to see the broad sweep of a river laid out before them.

It's almost as wide as the Nile. Flowing from east to west, it looks as though it's keeping to its banks, maybe even a bit lower than usual. It is summer here. The water is clear. Definitely not flooding. Susan gave her head a shake and chuckled. She hadn't realized how much river lore she had taken in while in Egypt. *There's not a palm tree in sight.* Susan sighed.

The horses stood in a small clearing. Katerina was already standing at the edge of the water. Watt lifted water for her so that she could dab at her face. Wetting her hands, she ran her fingers through her hair.

"Short, short," she muttered. "Grandmother will not be pleased." She quirked her face at Watt.

He shrugged. "We did what we needed to do," he said. "I think she will understand." He shook his head. "I hope she will understand."

Katerina laughed and twirled. "We're nearly there. We made it. Clean clothes. Safety."

Susan walked up beside her, still captured by the sight and smells of the wonderful river flowing beside her feet.

Katerina grabbed her hands.

"Thank you. Profoundly, I thank you," she said with a slight bow. "You will be rewarded."

Susan bowed back. "We're not there quite yet. But it looks wonderful. I'm eager to meet your grandmother. She sounds like a wise and courageous woman." Then Susan added, "What's this river called?"

Watt was the one who answered. Katerina was foraging in the bag tied to the back of her saddle.

"This is the River Rhine," he said. "It begins in the Alps and flows all the way through the Holy Roman Empire to the Northern Sea."

"It's a mighty river." Susan breathed in the fresh river smell.

Jason had stood quietly all this time, holding all the horses' reins and just looking. Susan noticed his stillness. *He looks dead on his feet.*

"Jason, are you all right?" She rested her hand on his shoulder.

He nodded. "Just a bit left out of the conversation is all." He stretched and prepared to mount Bunyip again.

Meanwhile, Watt had moved over to help Katerina with her bag, and as Susan turned, she saw that he was draping the beautiful blue cape around her shoulders. *It's looking a little the worse for wear,* Susan noticed.

Katerina mounted her horse and pulled the hood fully over her head so that her face was hidden. Watt spent time spreading the cape over the horse's rump so that it spread out in an almost regal way.

So, Susan thought, *we're back to images and family reputation. We're lucky she didn't want to stop and put on her dress.*

"Here we go, Myrtle. Last push before a warm stable and oats." Susan scrambled back into the saddle. She liked Myrtle, but she would be very glad not to have to ride her again.

The four of them picked their way through the willows back onto the road. It was much more crowded with travelers now. Mostly children but some adults as well. A nun led one group of children.

Their party didn't stop. They rode at a gentle canter down the center of the road, joining the throng eager to reach Cologne.

CHAPTER 24
COLOGNE

The city of Cologne itself was a different matter. Hundreds of children—*maybe even thousands,* Susan thought—thronged the streets. They sat in doorways, begged for food, scrapped among themselves, cried, laughed, sang. All of them seemed to have their attention fixed on the large cathedral on the hill. Many little feet were moving in that direction.

The adults in the street seemed mostly exasperated by the children. Many cuffed at the ones blocking their way. Other people, Susan saw, distributed food from baskets they carried.

The crowded streets soon meant that Susan's group had to dismount and lead their horses so they could keep moving.

Katerina led the way. She pulled her hood even closer around her face. Her steps were hurried as she jostled her way through the crowd. The others followed.

The lane they were following opened out into a large square. Tall wooden structures rimmed the four sides.

One building looked like a tavern. Soldiers spilled onto the square, standing, tankards in hand, watching the crowd. Others sprawled at little tables in the sunshine. The crowds seemed to amuse them.

A large crowd stood in the center of the square, their entire attention focused on a notice board. Soldiers stood to either side of the board. Arms folded across their chests, these soldiers glared down at the crowd. They were heavily armed. Susan looked around. Soldiers. Now that she took the trouble to look, she saw soldiers positioned all around the square. Others casually worked their way through the crowd.

Susan nudged Watt in the shoulder and, using her head, drew his attention to the soldiers. Watt nodded once quickly and moved up beside Katerina to whisper in her ear. She started and looked up quickly.

Just then, a man standing close to the notice jumped up onto the platform. He was young and well dressed. There was a lace trim at his cuffs, and a jaunty feather bobbed in his hat.

"I'll tell you what the notice says," he yelled to the crowd. "Otto's soldiers have taken over our city. That English bishop welcomed them in." He waved his arm toward the cathedral on the hill. He had more to say, but one of the soldiers on the platform clubbed him down with a fist to the side of his head. He toppled forward and fell heavily into the crowd. The people gasped and drew back. Some at the back hurried away. Others nearer the front pushed and shoved. They wanted to leave, too.

Katerina moved with the crowd. Head down, still leading her horse, she pushed through the people, heading for the road that led uphill from the square. Watt walked at her side. Susan tapped Jason on the shoulder. They pulled Myrtle and Bunyip into a walk and followed as closely as they could.

The crowd didn't care about them. People dodged around the four in their eagerness to get away from the square.

Soldiers cared, though. Katerina, with her head down and her hood pulled tight, bumped right into the chest of a soldier blocking her path.

The soldier grabbed her arm. He turned to the soldiers accompanying him. "Looky here. Weren't we told to look out for a splendid blue cloak?"

Other soldiers grabbed at Watt, Susan, and Jason. Susan stamped down hard on the foot of the soldier who grabbed her arms. He was wearing solid boots. She kicked at his shins. Shin guards. She thought of head butting him. Helmet. Susan stood quietly.

Watt turned to the soldiers with his hands out. "We're just stableboys who were hired to bring these horses into the city, sir," he said.

The soldier holding Katerina yanked the hood from her head. "Hmph, well, this doesn't look like the high and mighty Lady Katerina," he said, giving her a shake. "Stand still, lad," he added as Katerina started struggling and scowling and trying to bite.

Watt reached out to her. "Stay, Eric," he said. He turned again to the soldier in charge. "Sir, we know nothing about any lady. We brought these horses into the city for a merchant. We got the cloak off a girl on the way." Watt smirked suggestively at the soldiers.

"Don't care." The soldier in charge shrugged. "You might know something. You're coming with us."

The soldiers took the horses' reins and formed up around the four. They were marched out of the square.

Great, now I've been arrested, Susan thought. *Add that to scratched by a crocodile and sold to an orphanage. What adventures I do have.*

She hung her head, but she kept herself alert. She watched through her lashes. People glared from windows. A few stood in doorways, staring defiantly as the soldiers marched them past. One cluster of men standing in the street looked ready to attack. One man in particular started at the sight of their party. He bent quickly to a couple of his companions. He muttered something. One slapped him on the arm in agreement, and then he turned and scampered down the side street.

Their party was hustled through the crowds. The soldiers weren't gentle, but they weren't rough, either. Shortly, they turned onto a broad avenue. Ahead Susan saw a huge, elegant structure. As they drew nearer, Susan made out more detail. This building was constructed of stone. It wasn't a castle, though. It didn't have towers or those bumpy bits on the top of the walls, but it looked regal.

I guess that's a palace, Susan thought. *Maybe that's where Katerina's grandmother lives.*

Susan looked over at Katerina. Her shoulders were slumped. Her head hung low. Watt was looking around, alert and taking in everything he could.

Susan checked to see how Jason was doing. Not well. He was walking but only just. He looked exhausted. His face was pale, and his eyes were drooping. One of their soldier escorts held him by the arm, helping him along. Susan's heart sank with worry. *I'm supposed to be keeping him safe. I hope he's not getting sick again.*

The building had a grand entrance, and the avenue led right to the door. Above the door hung a solid carving in the shape of a shield. It was yellow, and a black bird, something like an eagle, was painted on it. The eagle's talons were long and sharp. Another shield covered the chest of the bird and this one showed three creatures drawn on it. They looked something like lions. The creatures were stacked one on top of the other.

Susan noticed a couple of men on either side of it. They were hanging on ropes from the roof. As their party neared the entrance, the two men above brought the carving crashing down into the roadway. A cheer went up from the roof, and a banner unfurled to cover the spot where the shield had been.

Katerina gasped, and Watt grabbed her arm and slowly shook his head.

Their party stopped. The leader rocked back on his heels. "Ah," he sighed. "Does me good to see the Welf banner in place." Susan squinted at the banner. Yellow background, black eagle, shield on its chest. Oh, the shield was a little smaller and only had two lions. *So little difference to be causing so much trouble.*

"Come on, you lot. Time to tell what you know." The soldiers marched the four into the Hohenstaufen palace, which now belonged to the Welfs. But where was Katerina's grandmother?

CHAPTER 25
THE PALACE

Katerina stopped dead in her tracks the moment she entered the main hall of the palace. Her face showed her shock. Eyes wide, mouth pressed tightly closed. The clenched fists at her side showed the boiling anger within. Susan moved beside her and touched her shoulder.

"Remember, Eric," she whispered. "We're just here to deliver horses."

Katerina jerked her head down in a quick nod. But her eyes roved the hall as the four stood in the doorway. Their soldier escort seemed uncertain of where to take them.

"Can anyone see the skinny guy? The one that's in charge of this place. The one that didn't run away." The head soldier looked around. "Big place."

He shuffled forward a few paces into the hall. Their escort pushed the four to follow.

The soldier holding Jason up jerked his head toward the head of the long table that dominated the room. "I think that's him over there, sir. The one in the red jerkin. The one pointing at the fireplace."

The head soldier nodded. "Go get him, son," he ordered.

The soldier pushed Jason in Susan's direction and took off across the hall to fetch the person who seemed to be in charge.

Susan caught Jason's arm. She raised her eyebrows in inquiry.

Jason nodded. "I'm just tired. And so very hungry. I figured why not let them haul me along. I didn't feel like helping them rush me to a questioning."

The two chuckled together.

Susan gave his shoulder a hug. *He always has an unusual way of looking at things.*

"So, what's going on here?" A loud, blustery voice interrupted Susan's thoughts.

The man in the red jerkin was standing in front of them, looking irritated and out of sorts.

"Why are you bothering me with four dirty boys?" he demanded.

To Susan's surprise, Katerina fell on her knees in front of the man.

"Oh, please, sir," she begged. "We're just stable-boys. We have to deliver horses to the Margrave of Bavaria. We cannot delay. We'll be punished."

The man took a step back and looked at Katerina at his feet. "I'm Griswald of the palace staff," he said. "Get up, boy." He used his foot to get Katerina to move.

She climbed slowly to her feet and stood quiet. She stared straight ahead and cocked her head a little to one side.

Griswald looked uncertain for a moment, and then he turned to the soldiers. "Did they have horses with them?"

The soldiers nodded. The head one offered, "We sent them around to the stables."

"Well, why have you dragged them in here then?" Griswald wanted to know.

The head soldier brought forward the blue cloak, which he had been holding. He explained their suspicions and why they wanted to hold the four for questioning.

Griswald took the cloak. He stroked the fabric as he slung it over his arm. Then he reached out and snatched Susan's bag from her shoulders. She grabbed at it, but Griswald was too quick for her.

"Right," he said. "I expect Sir Gustaff will want to try out all that new questioning equipment he had installed."

The head soldier squirmed a little. "Do you think that will be necessary, sir?" He waved at the four. "They seem good lads and haven't been much trouble."

"Nevertheless"—Griswald tugged his jerkin straight—"to the dungeon with them." He pointed to a small door leading off one side of the hall.

The soldiers prepared to set off with their captives.

"Wait." Griswald walked with them. "I know just the place to soften them up first." He chuckled and rubbed his hands. "Put them in the tar pit."

The soldiers stopped and looked around.

"Are you sure?"

"Yes, definitely." Griswald nodded. "It's the best place to get the information you need without much fuss." He sniggered behind his hand. "Nobody wants to spend time in the tar pit. They'll tell what they know."

"But we know nothing," Watt protested.

"Quiet, you." A soldier pushed him in the back. Soon they were moving across the grand and beautifully decorated hall, on their way to the dungeon to spend time in the tar pit.

Susan sighed. *Well, I've got out of locked rooms before. I guess I'll have to do it again. But a dungeon? Really? Come on, crystal. This is too much.*

Susan focused all her attention on remembering every twist and turn of their passage through the palace, down the steps, and into the dungeon.

The tar pit revealed itself as the last cell at the end of a long, damp tunnel. The door creaked with a loud shriek as the soldiers all pulled it open. The smell that wafted from the open door made Susan's nose sting. Jason made gagging noises.

The youngest soldier grabbed his nose. "I don't know, sir. I wouldn't keep my pig in there. Seems like there's other empty cells around here."

The head soldier shrugged. "I agree, but this is where he said to put them."

Susan looked around. There were plenty of other damp, dirty cells along the passage. None of them stank the way this one did. She hoped.

Turning back to the group, she saw that Katerina had already walked into the cell and pulled Watt in after her. Susan took a deep breath of relatively clean air and helped Jason in through the door.

The young soldier handed them a torch from the wall. "Here. Maybe having some light will help," he said.

And then the door slammed shut with a shriek.

CHAPTER 26
DUNGEONS STINK

Susan looked around their new home. It looked exactly like a trash dump. A big pile of rubbish lay in the middle of the room. Susan didn't want to think what could be in that pile. *Hope there isn't a body.* The thought sneaked out.

Katerina, Miss High-and-Mighty, walked quietly over to one wall and sat down with her back pressed against it and her knees drawn up to her chin. Watt stood near her. He looked unsure about what to do.

Susan helped Jason sit against the opposite wall. He slumped down. "I'm so hungry," he groaned.

"We'll never get out. They'll torture us. They won't believe we know nothing." Katerina started caterwauling at the top of her lungs. Susan stared at her in the light from the flickering torch. Katerina

152

looked back at her, still yelling at the top of her lungs and adding in big, loud sobs as well. But her hands were making motions like the conductor of an orchestra.

She wants me to do it, too? Susan raised her eyebrows and pointed at her chest.

Still yelling, Katerina nodded.

So Susan started yelling, too. "Oh, woe is us. We lost the horses." She got into the swing of things. "We're in so much trouble." More. More. "I want to go home."

Watt looked around and moved to try to comfort Katerina. She pushed him away and kept yelling and sobbing. He moved to comfort Susan, but she shook her head and shrugged.

Shaking his head, he sat against another wall.

Katerina eventually made motions with her hands that suggested that they could quiet down now. And so Susan tapered off her sobbing and screaming. *Huh. I felt like an Egyptian official mourner there for a moment.* Thoughts of her old companions, Tuthmoses and Djus, brought a soft smile to her face.

She stooped and slid down to sit against the back wall of the cell.

"Don't sit there," Katerina told her.

Surprised, Susan moved over to sit beside Jason.

Katerina scooched forward and started rummaging in the debris pile in the middle of the cell.

All Susan could do was watch, dumfounded.

With a sigh of satisfaction, Katerina uncovered a large metal box hidden below the mess. Watt helped her pull it clear.

It had no lock and opened easily. Food. Susan could smell food.

She slipped around the debris pile to have a closer look. Yes, Katerina pulled out a clay pot and quickly broke the wax seal around the lid.

Susan peered in. Katerina handed her a carrot. It was a bit limp and waggly, but it was a carrot. She took a bite. Lovely.

Katerina handed her another, and she took it across to Jason. She wiggled it under his nose, and his eyes flashed open.

"Food?" was all he said. He sat up and began munching happily.

"Make sure you chew it well before you swallow," Susan reminded him. *Fancy sounding like Mum at a time like this,* she added to herself.

Susan moved back to the box to see what else was on offer. Jason followed her, and they sat together so he could join the conversation.

Katerina had found a cloth in the box; it was now spread along the top, and food was laid out like a regular feast. There was a sort of dry cracker and a jar that held a chutney-type mixture. It spread on the crackers. Delicious. Susan popped one in her mouth and spread another. She had been trying to ignore the hunger she felt. But now, with food in front of her, she was ravenous.

The four ate in silence. Everything was delicious—perhaps not in twenty-first-century Canada. But here and now, it was a feast.

They finished off with apples. They had lost their crunch, but were sweet and tasty enough.

Finally Susan had had enough to eat. She sat back with a sigh. "This is the weirdest picnic I've ever been on," she said.

Jason nodded. "At least there's no ants."

"Thanks, Jason, now all I can think about is rats down here."

They both looked at Katerina, who was quietly folding up their tablecloth. She opened the box again, but instead of just stowing the cloth, she pulled on a loop at one end. It stuck. She stood and yanked harder. Watt peered into the box and tugged on another loop at the other end. Between them, they lifted out the floor of the box.

"A hidden compartment." Jason peered in.

"Of course." Susan chuckled.

"Weapons," Watt said and reached in.

Each piece was wrapped in cloth. "That's so they won't clank together and alert the guards," Katerina whispered.

Susan grinned over at Katerina. "That's why you yelled and screamed like that. In case the guards were listening at the door."

Katerina nodded with a smile and pulled out a long knife, which she handed to Susan. Susan accepted it but wasn't sure what to do with it.

Watt pulled out a sword and swung it around as though he was testing the weight and balance of it. He seemed satisfied and put it to the side. The next sword he drew out, he handed to Jason.

"Um." Jason hesitated. "Um, I've never wielded a sword. I'm sorry. I don't know how to use it."

Watt nodded. "Well, then," he said, "think of it as carrying a spare one for me in case I break mine."

He handed out belts, which had been under the weapons. Jason took one. Susan did, too. There was a sheath attached to it, and the knife fitted easily into it.

Katerina reached in again and pulled out one more sword. With a quirk of his head, Watt handed her a belt for it. "Here you are, Peter. Don't get it tangled in your legs."

"That's not the name we agreed was mine," Katerina said as she accepted the sword.

Watt shrugged and smiled. "Does it matter? I needed a boy's name for you, and I couldn't remember what we'd said before."

Susan chuckled quietly. "I can't remember what mine was, either," she said.

Jason clutched the sword and belt in his lap. "This has all been a bit of a surprise," he said. "The worst cell in the dungeon offers catering and weapons."

Katerina nodded with a smile. "Every family has to have hidden places of safety."

Jason moved a little apart from Susan. "Ours doesn't," he whispered to her.

Katerina moved back to the wall. "We should all get some sleep now. It's all we can do for the moment."

Watt shut the lid of the box, and Jason helped him pile all the rubbish back until it was well covered. They all settled down to sleep. Susan and Jason huddled together for warmth.

Susan felt her crystal digging into her thigh. *Yes, I could use you to get out, but that would be revealing what I can do. Let's see what happens first. Sleep is what I need.*

CHAPTER 27
SACRIFICE

Light flashing in her eyes woke Susan. She jolted upright to squint into the flame of a torch. She felt the heat from it. She put her arm up to shade her eyes.

In the flickering light, Susan saw that Watt stood, adjusting the sword belt around his waist.

Katerina was standing in the corner, speaking quietly to Griswald. He also held a lit torch in one hand; his arm was wrapped around Katerina's shoulders.

Susan turned to shake Jason awake but saw that Jason's eyes were open just a slit.

"It's OK," Susan whispered in his ear. "Looks as though these are Katerina's friends."

Jason sat up and stretched. "Right. I just thought I'd lie doggo until I knew what was going on."

Susan poked him in the ribs. "What, now you're going to start talking in another language?"

Jason shrugged as he stood. "Sorry, guess a little Australian slipped in there."

He busied himself trying to figure out how to get the sword belt around his waist so that the sword hung correctly along his right hip. Once he was satisfied with how it sat, he experimented with drawing the sword. He tried to get the sword out of its scabbard with his right hand. It didn't work.

Watt walked over, chuckling. He put his right hand across his body and pulled his sword out of the scabbard on his left side. "You really haven't ever carried a sword before." He observed. "Don't worry about it now. I'll teach you on the road. Help me move the box out." Watt pulled the metal box from under the debris pile.

Jason grabbed the other end, and the two lifted it. That's when Susan, who had been watching all this, noticed that the fourth wall of the cell—the one Katerina had told her not to lean against—now had a wide opening in it.

Watt and Jason had to stand to one side as four men entered the cell. Each carried a body in his arms. They gently laid the bodies down beside the debris. Susan bent to look closely. The first she examined was the body of a young boy about her age and size. She could see an awful gash in his side. The boy was so pale that Susan concluded that he must have lost a lot of blood before he died.

"This is Hans…was Hans."

Startled, Susan looked up into the sad face of the man who had carried in the body…Hans. "What happened?" she asked.

The man straightened Hans out into a more comfortable position, as though he could still feel. "Welfs happened," he said.

Susan stood. She looked around. Four dead boys. Laid out on the floor. Dressed much as they were.

The man stood also. "Hans." He pointed to the boy at their feet. "Varin." He pointed to another. "Mintho and Poncet." He pointed to the other two. "All good boys." Tears ran freely down the man's cheeks. "All killed in the last week as the Welfs took Cologne."

"How? Why?"

The man looked over at Susan and smiled a tight smile. "They were celebrating the election of Frederick as emperor. They were friends. Apprentices. But Welfs had sneaked into the city ahead of Otto's marauders, and they cornered the four in an alley. The boys were weaponless, but they fought with their knives. It was all over before we could rally to the area. But they managed to severely wound one of their attackers, and we learned much from him—before he died."

Susan shuddered. "Why have you brought them here, though?"

"Their last service to Emperor Frederick II will be to stand in for you as you make your escape."

"But they don't look anything like us." Susan was puzzled.

Jason came up beside her. "Took me a while to work it out," he said. "We've taken out the metal box. Look how much flammable material there is in this room. One torch in that pile in the middle of the floor, and this cell and everything in it is gone."

"But that will burn down the palace. Seems a bit drastic."

Watt joined them. He waved his hand around the cell. "Stone," he said. "All stone. Except for the door and that's metal. The palace is safe."

Watt pulled them toward the gap in the wall. Everyone crowded into the tunnel beyond.

Griswald offered his torch to Katerina. "Would you like to have the honor, m'lady?"

Katerina took the torch. She squared her shoulders. For a moment, she squinted into the room.

"I honor you, Hans, Varin, Mintho, and Poncet. Thank you for your sacrifice," she said and threw the burning torch onto the heap of debris in the middle of the room. It caught quickly, and for a moment, they watched the flames light the entire cell.

The men put their shoulders to a wheel fastened to the wall where they stood. With a thud, a stone doorway covered the hole. They all took a moment to breathe the fresher air of the tunnel.

I'd forgotten how stinky that cell was. Susan took another, very relieved, deep breath.

CHAPTER 28
A LONG, DARK TUNNEL TO...

In the flickering torchlight, Susan had a chance to check out their surroundings. They stood in a narrow tunnel. The walls were roughly hewn, and the rock beneath her feet felt bumpy when she scuffed her shoe. Nine people made up their group. The four travelers, the four men who had carried in the boys' bodies, and Griswald.

Gone was the elegant, sneering courtier they had first encountered. Now he looked like a kindly grandfather. He turned to Katerina and gave her a huge hug, and she hugged him back. Griswald was the first to pull back. He held Katerina by the shoulders and smiled down into her face.

"Let me look at the boy you for a moment longer." He shook his head. "You can't imagine how astounded I was to hear the code phrase from the mouth of a shabby boy." He chuckled. "What were you thinking?"

Katerina waved her hand. "It works. Sir Gustaff has been turning the countryside upside down looking for us, and yet here we are."

"Hmm, yes, here you are. In our dungeon."

"I'll be in my grave if Gustaff and his family catch me," Katerina retorted. "Where's Lady Beatrice? I need to talk to her urgently."

"Ah, Lady Beatrice wished to begin arrangements for Frederick's crowning and also to sway the good people of Lake Konstanz to his cause. She has moved there."

Katerina tensed up in frustration. "I must travel there immediately," she said. "It's so urgent. Frederick is in danger, and I must get a warning to him."

Griswald threw up his hands. "Don't tell me." He wagged his finger. "I have to stay here and work quietly to keep our people safe and do what I can against these infernal Welfs."

As they talked, the entire troop moved along the tunnel. They stopped when they reached stone steps cut into one side. They led up into darkness.

"I have to go." Griswald waved at the steps. "I have to go up there and be indignant about the dungeon being in flames. Henri is waiting with a fast boat. I intended to send you to your grandmother anyway." He rubbed his chin and smiled. "Although not in such disarray." He picked up a bundle that was lying on the bottom step. "I gathered together what I could from your chests. I hope this will help with your comfort," he said.

"And I have this empty sack here," he added. "It seemed important, so I brought it along." He swung Susan's bag from his finger.

A wave of relief swept over Susan. A huge grin stretched her cheeks. All the things that Mrs. Coleman had given her plus a few she had added herself. She had it again. She grabbed it and slung it across her shoulders. The familiar weight on her hip felt wonderful.

Then she remembered her manners. She bobbed a curtsey to Griswald. "Thank you, sir," she said.

He shook his head. "Another girl, no less," he said. "Good luck to you, my dear."

He turned to leave. He hadn't gone more than two steps before Katerina caught his arm.

"Wait," she said. "One of the Welfs gave us a torch so we would have light," she said. "He seemed young and kind, and he is going to get blamed for this."

Griswald nodded. "Sounds like a good recruit. I'll do what I can." He turned and ran up the stairs.

Everyone took a deep breath and then continued the slog along the tunnel.

Susan was bursting with questions. She grabbed Jason's hand, and together they moved up behind Katerina.

Where to start?

"Why did you tell Griswald about the boy who gave us a torch?" Probably not the most important question but the one on the tip of her tongue.

Katerina kept walking, but she cocked her head to one side. "We have learned that most men are not vicious and brutal naturally. We observed that even a good man, if made to perform enough dishonorable, cruel acts, will become hardened." She hitched up the bag on her shoulder. "Once they become that way, there is little chance of them turning back to the path of honor. They get worse and worse. It seems to be a downhill slope." Katerina shrugged. "That boy helped us. He was probably born into a Welf-controlled village and was made to take up arms. There seemed hope for him still."

Susan noticed Watt was listening to the conversation.

"It's like Sir Gustaff," Watt said. "His father encouraged him to beat servants as soon as he could walk. He had the example of his father's brutality, too. He's never thought past it." He turned around to face them, walking backward. "And then there's

Sir Klaus. He's not brave, so he hangs around Gustaff, agrees with everything he says, and hopes for favor."

Katerina nodded. But Watt wasn't finished.

"And then there's Sir Robert."

Katerina harrumphed, but Watt forged on.

"Sir Robert. Sent by his king to support the emperor Otto, his nephew. What does he do? He's an honorable man who finds himself in a dishonorable situation. He owes his allegiance to King John, who orders him to remain. Now there's a man torn." Having said his piece, Watt turned and hurried to catch up with the leading men.

Katerina swiped at her face with her sleeve.

To distract her, Susan hunted for another question. "Who's Henri?"

Katerina sniffed and squared her shoulders. "Henri is Griswald's son," she said. "He used to play tag with me when I was younger." She sighed. "It will be good to see him again."

"So he's got a boat?" Susan wanted to keep her talking.

"Yes," Katerina answered. "Well, actually it's our boat, but not many know that. It plies the river in trade but is useful for moving things along the river discreetly. There's always secrets in politics."

Just like in Egypt, the river is important to the life of the people, Susan realized.

Jason had the next question. "So where are we going now?"

Katerina turned back to look at him. "Sometimes you speak, and other times you're silent?" Her expression made the statement a question.

"Um, I'm learning as fast as I can." Jason looked at her. "So where are we going?"

"To Lake Konstanz to find Grandmother, the Lady Beatrice."

"On a boat?" Jason asked.

Katerina nodded. "It's up the River Rhine. We will be rowing toward the Alps."

Jason sighed. "Here comes some blisters."

Katerina chuckled. "You won't have to row. We have workers for that."

Susan was relieved to see that Katerina seemed happier. They were moving along the tunnel at quite a fast pace. She had no sense of how far they had walked, but it felt like a long way. There had been other side tunnels as they had moved along, but now the way ahead was straight and smooth. She slid one hand along the wall. It didn't feel like stone—more like clay—and she noticed water flowed along a groove carved in the floor.

"This is a very long tunnel," she puffed.

Katerina nodded. "It would be longer still, except it was dug from the end of the row of dungeons."

"How much farther?" Jason wanted to know.

Katerina shrugged. "I don't know. I've never been down here before."

One of the leaders turned back toward them. "Not much farther now, m'lady," he said.

In about a hundred more paces, a doorway led them into a large room. Wooden crates were stacked neatly against one wall, and barrels covered another. Here, the floor was flagged with flat stones and the walls were dry. A set of steps, leading up, occupied one wall. Susan sank down on a box, slipped off her shoes, and rubbed her right foot. It felt soooo good. She felt as though she'd walked miles.

Noise filtered into the room. People, many people, were walking around upstairs. Susan looked at the ceiling; dust motes seeped through and drifted down, sparkling in the torchlight.

"We're in the cellar of the Cod and Eel, m'lady." One of the men bowed to Katerina.

"Thank you, Rylan." She inclined her head in acknowledgment.

Bang. The door at the top of the stairs opened. *Thump.* Footsteps rattled down the steps. Gradually a person was revealed. *Thump.* Bare feet. *Thump, thump.* The hem of a skirt with a petticoat showing. *Thump, thump, thump.* More of a bright-red skirt. An empty jug swung from the hands of this person. *Thump* and the person jumped the last two steps and came face-to-face with a cluster of four strong men, all looking at her.

The girl shrieked.

"Now that's enough, Bridgette. You know it's us," Rylan said, laughing.

"Ooh, I near dropped me jug." Bridgette held her hand to her heart. "Came for more wine, I did. Sir Mucky-Muck is up there. Give us yer best, he said. Then he thumped me backside." Bridgette gave her backside a rub. "Then he laughed."

Bridgette stalked across the cellar to one of the wine barrels. She pulled on the spigot to start wine flowing into her jug.

"I want them Welfs gone. You hear? Gone." She thrust her hands on her hips. "They stink up the place. Like as not, he won't even pay. Smash things up if he doesn't get the best." She stopped the spigot and lifted the jug into her arms. "Arrogant. Rude. That's them. Get them gone and hurry up about it." She stomped over to the stairs.

"Oh." She turned. "Henri is upstairs waiting for ya." She climbed a couple of steps. "I'll tell him you're here, shall I?" And she ran the rest of the way to the top.

Rylan took a deep breath and chuckled. "She's getting saucier and saucier."

"What happens now?" Susan asked.

"We wait," Rylan replied, making himself comfortable on another box.

One of the other men picked up a jug he found standing on a table. He walked over to the line of wine barrels. "This was the good one, wasn't it?" he asked with a grin.

Everyone nodded. Susan got up and went looking for wine cups on the table.

CHAPTER 29
THE BOAT

They all found places to sit on a box or on the floor. The men obviously enjoyed the wine, emptying their cups and refilling them from the jug. Susan supposed it was good; she still sort of screwed up her face at the sourness of it. In Egypt she had often had wine but mixed with a lot of water. She could find no water in the cellar. She and Jason sipped delicately from their cups.

Katerina sat quietly beside them. She also sipped her wine. Watt prowled around the cellar. *He looks caged*, Susan noticed.

Watt picked up a bag he found lying on the table among the cups. He shook it and peered inside. He turned it upside down and gave it a good shake. Straw sprinkled down, but nothing fell out. He picked up four cups from the table; he found a knife there. He tested the blade. From his expression, he wasn't impressed but popped it in the bag anyway. He kept searching the table.

Susan hugged her bag. Griswald had said it was empty. It didn't feel empty. She hoped everything was there. She peered in, but in the flickering torchlight, she couldn't see. It wouldn't be a good idea to start pulling everything out. There were things in there that hadn't been invented yet, and it was best to keep them secret if possible. Susan couldn't resist thrusting her hand in, though—just to feel familiar things.

But not everything was familiar. Her hand rested on a small bag; it felt like soft leather and clinked when she moved it. Drawing it out into the light, Susan saw that she was holding a black money purse. She gave it a shake. It rattled.

Katerina turned with a smile. "Was that in your bag?"

Susan nodded.

Katerina held up hers. "He slipped one to me when we hugged," she said. "Griswald always made sure I had enough money whenever I left the palace." She added, "I hope he will be safe."

Katerina showed Susan how to thread the purse onto her belt. They had to stand to make the necessary adjustments, and they were still standing when the commotion started upstairs.

A chair scraped harshly across the floor. A man roared in anger. A chair toppled over. Feet moved around, getting louder and louder. More yelling. More stomping.

Rylan and his companions stood and began gathering their things together. They drained their wine cups and clustered at the bottom of the stairs.

The stomping and shouting continued above.

The door at the top of the stairs opened quietly.

A head appeared. "Coming?"

The group needed no further urging, and all hurried up the stairs. Rylan, in the lead, greeted the person at the door.

"Henri, good to see you." They clasped forearms. Rylan nodded toward the clatter and noise. "Bridgette spilled the wine?"

Henri laughed. "Nope, this time she hit him with the jug—still pretended to trip, though."

Rylan shook his head with a laugh. "She is getting way too good at that."

The group slipped out of the cellar and skirted along the wall of the taproom. Sturdy chairs were being thrown. Men were jostling and pushing at one another. As she slipped out the front door of the Cod and Eel, Susan looked back into the melee. There was Bridgette, standing on a table, wielding her jug. There was a lot of noise and stamping, but nobody seemed to be getting hurt.

The door of the tavern shut behind her, and Susan stood on a darkened street in Cologne. She could smell the river. They were close. The wooden buildings leaned over the narrow street. A few houses had torches burning near their front doors, but mostly the streets were dark.

Their group slipped quietly down to the riverfront.

The boat was tied to a dock built along the riverbank. Susan could see little in the dark. They slipped up the gangplank and were no sooner on board than mooring ropes were untied and the boat drifted away from the bank.

Rowers grasped their oars and dipped them to the rhythm of rowing. The boat took to the river, making barely a sound.

Jason came up beside her. "Imagine trying to make a quiet get away in a motorboat." Susan shoulder bumped him, and they moved back to join the rest of the group.

Rylan and Henri were explaining to Katerina that they would tie up to the bank soon. It was not safe to travel on the river at night. They had a mooring spot planned just ahead.

They reached a spot where they could see a pattern of flaming torches set out along the bank. Two stationary flames marked the safe area for the boat, and the waving one showed by the pattern it wove that this was their planned spot.

"More boats move on the river at night than you would think," Henri explained.

"Smugglers?" Katerina asked.

Henri nodded. "And a few pirates."

Jason sighed. "That's just great." Susan squeezed his hand.

Katerina lay down on the deck. Soft mats had been spread for them. "We are on our way to Lady Beatrice," she said quietly. "Our ordeal is almost over." She sighed and turned over to go to sleep.

Susan grabbed Jason's hand and pulled him off to one side.

"We must stay together," she whispered to him. "If Katerina's troubles are almost done, and we've altered the imbalance, the crystal will pull me home, and you will need to come with me."

Jason looked around. "I'll miss all this," he said. "It's scary, but so is having cancer. At least here I can do something about the scary. At home, I'm just sick, and the doctors do the stuff."

Susan had never thought of it like that. She gave him a big hug. "You're amazing," she told him.

They settled down to sleep in a cluster with the others. But Susan made sure that her hand was on Jason's arm. After all, there had been times when the crystal had taken her places while she slept.

CHAPTER 30
THE RIVER

Travel on the River Rhine quickly fell into a routine. Wake at dawn. Eat a hearty breakfast. Pack up their camp. Launch the boat and move farther up the river toward Lake Konstanz.

Throughout the long summer days, the rowers worked in shifts to keep the boat moving into the current. Some days, if the wind was right, they hoisted a sail and the rowers rested. Susan counted her paces along the wooden deck – about thirty-five of her paces from bow to stern. *This whole boat would fit in mum's studio.*

Susan spent a lot of her time gazing at the passing fields and forests. They passed many small villages and even a few towns. She saw travelers moving along roadways in some places. Some rode mules or donkeys. Horses were popular, too, but seemed to be limited to the richer travelers.

That's why we pretended to be four boys delivering hors-es, she realized.

Most of the people she saw walked. They pulled carts with their possessions if they were lucky. She saw few bridges. Most people crossed the river on small ferryboats.

Many boats plied the waters around them. Some were local fishing boats, while others looked to be carrying trade goods up and down the river. The crew of their boat acknowledged many of the others as though they were friends or even family.

Katerina and Susan maintained their disguise as boys. Any passing boat that saw a lady on board would be sure to speak of it downriver. They want-ed the Welfs to think they had died in the dungeon fire.

As dusk drew in at the end of each long sum-mer's day, the boat would pull into the shore. In many places, river stones were set into the bank, which allowed the boat to be drawn partly out of the water. Susan learned that the bow was rein-forced with metal to allow this beaching without causing damage. In some places, the riverside had been created as a business, and people would be waiting to help them move ashore, and food would be ready for them.

Sort of like a riverside motel, Susan thought with a grin.

The River Rhine was a hustling, bustling place. Long, twisty, and busy.

━┿ ┿━

Days on the river soon blended together. People fell into routines. Work got done. People ate, slept, drank, and rowed. Susan and Katerina never rowed, but they found other tasks that kept them busy, too.

Watt, true to his promise, spent time with Jason each evening, teaching him the art of swordsmanship as dusk gathered over their camp. Susan sometimes fell asleep with the clang of their swords ringing in her ears. She was happy for Jason; he was having the time of his life. He could speak the language quite fluently now and didn't need to be gripping her hand to understand what was going on. He laughed a lot. The summer sun had tanned his skin and bleached his hair. Jason moved with a new fluid grace. It was wonderful to see. Susan worried a little at what the consequences would be when the crystal took them home. Would he be sick then? How would they explain the physical changes? It was all a puzzle.

Even though they traveled in comfort along the river, Susan felt certain there was more danger in store for them. Katerina must still be in danger; otherwise the crystal would have taken them home.

At night, Katerina usually shared a tent with Susan. Some nights they chatted long after they blew out their candles. Katerina enjoyed the freedom of acting the boy, and she liked blending in with the group.

Only Henri knew who Katerina was. Rylan had returned to Cologne after the first night. The crew knew she was a Hohenstaufen, and that she had escaped from the palace dungeons. They knew it was important to get this person to Lady Beatrice quickly, and all knew that it had something to do with besting the Welfs and placing the correct emperor, Frederick, on the throne.

One crew member paid particular attention to the four. Susan noticed that Drust singled Katerina out for special attention, bringing her choice meat from the cooking pits and fetching her a blanket in the cool of the evening. Katerina took these little attentions for granted, as though they were her due.

They settled on Peter as Katerina's name and Eric for Susan. It became second nature to Susan to respond to that name. She was comfortable as Eric.

Susan, Merit-Amen, Eric. What's in a name? I am all of these. I am me, whatever I'm called. How many more will I have? Susan thought about it one day as she strolled along the river path. They had beached the boat for the night. Their tent was set up, but the meal wasn't ready yet. There were two other boats already in place, so the camp was quite crowded this night.

Susan took the opportunity to take a walk and catch her breath.

The river was particularly beautiful in this area. And Susan was enjoying the quiet, away from everyone.

"Hey, wait up." Jason came running along the path toward her.

She turned to watch him come. As he ran, he used one hand to prevent his sword from slapping his leg. His strides were easy and comfortable. His face lit with a huge grin.

He looks as though he was born with that sword on his hip, Susan observed.

"Your dueling lessons are going well," she said as Jason caught up to her.

Jason nodded. "It's good exercise," he said. "I like the logic of it."

They turned and continued along the riverbank.

"I just hope I never have to actually use the sword to fight. I don't want to hurt anyone, you know." Jason shook his head.

Susan skipped a step and looked over at him. "I understand." She nodded. "It's like they take the fighting and killing for granted. And if you're a lord, you can kill who you like, and everyone shrugs."

Jason shuddered. "Scary times."

They walked on, each thinking their own thoughts.

They came to a bend in the river. On the opposite bank, the water had carved into the land, forming a cliff, and on their side, it had spread out, making a marshy area. Susan heard ducks quacking in the reeds.

"Let's go around the marsh and head back through the forest," she suggested.

The two of them picked their way through the mud to higher ground and headed back to camp along a narrow path through the woods. The path suddenly opened out into a little clearing.

Surprised, they stopped. Across the glade stood a cluster of men. Four of them with their heads together, talking quietly, almost whispering. Dressed as crewmen in sturdy leggings and woolen tunics, the four sprang apart as soon as they became aware of Jason and Susan. One of the men was Drust. Susan caught just a glimpse of him before he covered his face and hurried away through the trees.

The other three stared at the two.

Susan and Jason stood for a moment. Susan glanced around the clearing. It seemed to her that something wasn't right here. She tugged at Jason's arm. "Look like you belong," she said out of the corner of her mouth. Susan gripped her crystal in her pocket. She held Jason's arm. The two of them walked casually across the clearing toward the men.

"Good evening." Susan nodded to the men as they passed.

The men muttered a courtesy back.

Susan's back prickled, but she didn't turn She wanted to rub the back of her neck to peel off their eyes. She listened for the slightest sound of movement from the men. That would be the first sign that they were going to attack. But the men stayed in place.

Once more among the trees and out of sight of the three men, Susan let out a relieved sigh.

"That was weird," Jason observed. "What do you think was going on?"

Susan shrugged. "It could be nothing, but they acted suspiciously. That puts my danger antenna up."

"Huh?"

"Well, I think there's more danger," Susan added. "After all, we're still here. We haven't settled the imbalance yet."

"I've been thinking about that," Jason responded. "We've saved Katerina a couple of times. We've been tagging along on this adventure. I guess we have to make sure she gets to Lake Konstanz and saves her cousin so he will be crowned emperor."

Susan nodded.

"What if Cousin Frederick is a really bad guy and is going to make a terrible emperor and this Otto guy is the one who would be a good emperor?"

They stopped in their tracks and looked at each other.

Susan slowly shook her head. "I don't think it works like that. The crystal takes me to places where I can fix an imbalance."

They moved on in silence for a while.

"I have to believe that the crystal is getting me to work for good."

They walked a bit farther.

"I wouldn't be able to do this if I didn't think I was working for good."

Jason caught her arm and pulled Susan into a big hug. "You really are a wonderful person, Susan," he said. "I always feel so safe with you. Even through all these hairy adventures, you make me feel safe. I believe you will always find the good in whatever situation you get us into."

The hug felt wonderful to Susan. Tension drained out of all parts of her. Her heart slowed. She breathed deeply and let it out slowly. She hadn't realized how tense and worried she was. *That's Jason. None of that silly stuff about boys not being able to say nice things to girls. He isn't afraid to be himself.*

Finally she pulled away. "Oh, so you're coming on other adventures with me, are you?"

Jason gave a solemn nod. "I hope so," he said. "Someone has to keep you safe," he added.

Susan sniffed the air. "Food," she said.

"Smells like meat tonight. Good, I'm hungry. Smells like barbecue." Jason took a deep breath. "Race you back," he yelled, already two paces ahead.

Susan hurried to catch up, and they soon made it back to camp. Sure enough, the meal was ready.

CHAPTER 31
DRUST

"What's this meat?" Jason asked Watt.

"Venison," Watt answered.

Jason looked puzzled.

Uh-oh, a word he hasn't heard before. Susan supplied the answer. "It's deer," she told him.

Jason dropped the piece he was eating. "Not Bambi?"

Susan patted his arm, laughing. "No, no, not movie Bambi, he was a North American deer."

"Well, OK then." Jason picked up his trencher and took another big bite of the meat. "Tasty."

"Who's Bambi?" Watt wanted to know.

Jason patted him on the shoulder. "Sort of a childhood friend."

Susan and Jason put their heads together for a quiet chuckle.

"Sometimes I just don't understand you two," Watt declared and marched over to the other side of the fire where Katerina sat in deep conversation with Henri.

Susan watched him go. He dropped onto the seat on the other side of Henri. And that was when Susan noticed Drust. He sat as close as he possibly could to the group. He had his back to them, but he was leaning away from his table so that he was almost touching Henri. His head was cocked to one side and every fiber of his body strained towards where Katerina and Henri chatted. *He's listening. He's spying.*

Susan's quick gasp led Jason to follow her gaze, and he immediately saw the same thing.

He jumped up. "Time to join the party, I think," he said, straightening his sword belt on his hip.

Susan stood, too. "You're right."

Susan slipped onto the bench opposite Drust, and Jason crowded onto the bench next to him. Their feet touched under the table.

"Why hello, Drust," Susan said sweetly. "Why did you rush off so quickly in the forest?"

"We would have liked to meet your friends, you know," Jason added.

Drust shied away from Jason only to be face-to-face with Susan. She looked at him with eyebrows raised. They had succeeded in drawing all Drust's attention away from Katerina and Henri's conversation. But Susan wanted more.

"Oh, urm, uh, they're my cousins," Drust stammered.

"Well, all the more reason to meet them." Susan looked around to see if she could see them anywhere around the area.

"No, no." Drust grabbed her hand on the table. "Their captain is very strict." Drust shook his head. "They are not allowed to, um…they're not allowed to speak with the other crews." Drust shook his head and sighed. He lowered his voice to a whisper. "I think they might do a bit of smuggling, you know?"

"Huh." Susan stood up on the bench and looked all around. Sure enough, over in one corner on the set of tables farthest from the fire, she saw the three men from the forest. They were huddled around a table with other men. They all turned to look at her.

"They seem very interested in me," Susan declared, putting her hands on her hips.

"Yes, Eric." Katerina turned in her seat. She waved her hand. "Everyone seems to be interested in the boy standing on the seat. Are you going to sing or something?"

Susan scrambled down. "No, that won't be necessary." She felt her face glowing red.

Katerina stood and stretched. "Well, it's time to sleep anyway." She patted Henri's shoulder. "Good night, Captain," she said. "Coming, Eric?" She flipped her head toward their tent.

Susan grabbed a candle from the table and fell into step beside her. They ambled through the camp until they reached their tent. They stooped to enter.

Once they were tucked up under their blankets on their cots, Susan broached the subject that was most worrying her.

"How well do you know Drust?"

Katerina turned on her side so they were facing each other. Her brows were slightly wrinkled. "I don't know him at all." Katerina shook her head. "I can't remember ever seeing him around the palace, but then, I've been gone from there for quite a while, so he could have joined the staff after I left. He's been helpful."

Katerina moved to blow out the candle.

"Wait, don't blow it out yet." Susan put her hand out to stop Katerina. "Let me tell you what I saw." And so Susan told Katerina, in whispers, about Jason's and her forest encounter. She also told Katerina about his explanation of what had been happening.

By the time Susan had finished her tale, the two of them were sitting on their cots with their heads close together.

Katerina shrugged, though. "That seems right to me," she whispered. "All these river people seem to know one another and are often related. It's a pretty tight-knit group. There's a lot to know about traveling on the Rhine, and they keep that knowledge in the families." She fluffed up her blankets, ready to lie down again. "He's been helpful and attentive to me since we've been on the river. He even offered to lend me his comb when he saw me washing my hair." Katerina yawned. "I'll ask Henri about him tomorrow morning." Katerina yawned again, but before she could snuggle under her blanket, the girls heard a knife tapping on the side of a jug.

After a momentary start, Susan relaxed. How else do you knock on a tent?

"Peter?" It was Drust.

"Um, yes," Katerina answered.

"I've brought you some mulled wine. There's a chill in the air tonight, and I thought you might like it."

Katerina looked at Susan. Susan shrugged. "You can come in, Drust," Katerina answered.

Drust pushed through the tent flap and stood at the end of their cots.

"Eric." Drust nodded to acknowledge Susan. "I know that you were wondering about my family earlier," he said. Although he was talking to Susan, all his attention was focused on Katerina. "I'm sorry if my cousins caused you alarm," he added. "They're a rough lot, and once my mother married into their clan, it was hard for me." He set two cups down on their stool and poured the mulled wine. It smelled delicious. Susan could sense a wine base, but there was the scent of lemons, too. A faint whiff of cinnamon floated on the air.

Katerina inclined her head. "Thank you, Drust," she said. "That was a kind thought. Just leave the jug, and we will bring it out in the morning."

Drust nodded to them. He picked up the two cups and held them out. "Here you go." He smiled. "Get this inside you. It's just the right temperature. You don't want to let it get cold."

The girls took the cups. Katerina sniffed hers to get the full aroma. "Wonderful." She breathed in the malty, spicy tang and downed the drink in one gulp. Susan sipped hers.

Susan took another sip. Drust refilled Katerina's cup.

"Thank you." Katerina nodded. "This is tasty. There's some flavor in it that I'm not familiar with. What is it?"

"Um." Drust moved toward the tent flap with his jug. "It's a family secret," he mumbled. "I'll bid you a good night's sleep," he said and left.

Katerina shook her head. "Strange little man." She yawned and placed her empty cup on the ground.

Susan was surprised to see she had emptied her cup as well. She felt warm and relaxed and very comfortable.

Katerina leaned over and blew out the candle. "Good night," she said. "I feel wonderfully relaxed. I think I will sleep well this night."

"Good night," Susan mumbled, already half-asleep.

CHAPTER 32
WHERE'S KATERINA?

Susan was never sure what woke her in the night. Gradually she realized that she couldn't hear Katerina breathing.

Susan lay in the dark. Her head felt muzzy and heavy, and her eyes didn't want to open. But something was nagging at her. Where was Katerina?

Probably had to go to the latrine, she thought and snuggled under her blanket.

Then she sat bolt upright. "We have a chamber pot," she mumbled.

She spread her hands across the cot opposite. No Katerina.

She stood and groped her way to the tent flap. "Katerina," she called. As soon as she was standing in the brisk night air, her head began to clear. She took a couple of deep breaths and let them out slow-ly. *Calm down*, she told herself. *It's probably nothing.*

"Peter." Susan began walking through the sleep-ing camp. "Peter." She kept calling but not too loudly. She didn't want to wake the entire camp and attract undue attention to Katerina if she was just staring at the stars or something.

Her wanderings took her down toward the riv-er. As she drew near the bank, she became aware of a scraping sound. *That's a boat being launched*, she realized.

Running now, she breasted the ridge that sepa-rated the camp from the river. Yes, men were push-ing a boat into the river. It seemed too early to be starting out. The river was dangerous and hard to navigate at night, wasn't it?

Several torches were lit along the bank to ease the crew's launching efforts. One man stood out from all the others. He directed the men and en-sured that the launch was going smoothly. When he moved close to one of the torches, Susan saw his face fully lit. Drust's cousin. Well, Drust had suggested they were smugglers.

The captain walked over to a small man standing to one side, watching the proceedings. He put his hand on the smaller man's shoulder, and as soon as Susan's attention was drawn to that figure, she saw it was Drust.

And all the questions clicked in her head to an answer. She turned and ran. Back into the camp. Which tent was Watt and Jason's? Where was Henri sleeping?

"Help, help," she yelled as she ran. "Peter is being kidnapped." She heard groans as people woke. But it was not fast enough. She began shaking tent walls as she ran. "Hurry, hurry," she yelled at the top of her voice. "Peter. Peter is in danger!"

Henri grabbed her arm. "Stay still a moment. What are you saying?"

Susan took a deep breath and pointed toward the river. "It's Peter, Peter," she cried. "He's being kidnapped." She jumped up and down with impatience. "Quickly, quickly, the boat is leaving. I'm sure they have Peter."

"Did you see Peter on the boat?"

"No, no, but he's not in the tent. I woke. Hurry, hurry, the boat is leaving."

Henri turned to one of his men who had joined them. "Serrill, get to the river. See what's happening there."

The man nodded and ran for the river.

Henri turned back to Susan. "Take a deep breath. What makes you think that she has been taken?"

Susan did take a moment to breath. "Isn't it odd for a boat to be leaving in the middle of the night?" She asked her own question.

Jason came up beside her.

Henri nodded. "Yes." He shrugged. "Smugglers, you know."

"So." Susan fanned her face with her hand. "Wouldn't smugglers do anything to get a reward? Wouldn't they kidnap someone if they had heard that a certain ex-emperor's family were looking for a person who could be here with us? Wouldn't they watch for their chance?"

Henri frowned. He turned Susan's face to the light of a torch. "Are you feeling all right?" he asked. "You look a little dazed."

Susan shook her head and then groaned. "The fact that I have a thumping headache isn't important right now. Peter is missing, and I think he's being taken out on the river on that boat that I saw leaving."

At that moment, Serrill returned. He was panting hard. "Eric is correct," he said with a nod toward Susan. "The boat has slipped away."

"Which boat?" Henri wanted to know.

"The Derrin family boat."

Henri nodded. "They're Welfs." He looked worried. "Search the camp for Peter. Prepare our boat to move. If we cannot find Peter, we will go in pursuit."

Men started running in all directions to gather up their gear and to search more closely for Peter.

But Serrill, bowed again, even lower. "There's more, Captain," he said.

Henri sighed and turned to him. "What else could there be?"

Serrill gulped. "Our boat is floating in the stream. It's been pushed into the river."

Henri put his hand to his heart. "Who was on watch?" he demanded.

"Drust," one of the men piped up. "He asked for the duty."

"Drust!" Jason interjected. "That settles it. Tell them, Eric."

Quickly, in gasping breaths, Susan told of the chance meeting with Drust and his cousins in the forest. Jason chipped in, too, with more of the tale, telling about the way Drust seemed to be listening to them talking and what he had said in explanation.

But then Susan had to come back in to the tale and explain about the mulled wine Drust had brought.

During the telling, Henri's face grew sterner and sterner.

When Susan had finally finished her story, Henri turned her face to the torch. He peered closely into her eyes. The torch dazzled, but Susan tried to keep her eyes open. She just wanted to run to the river.

"You look as though you've been drugged. What was in the wine?"

Susan slumped to the ground. "Peter drank twice as much as I did," she whispered. "Drust said it was a secret family recipe."

Henri nodded to her once. "Let's move." He turned to his men. "Get a boat. Get ours back ashore. We're giving chase. Move."

And move they did. Most running for the river's edge.

Another captain hurried over to Henri.

"My crew is at your disposal to help retrieve your vessel," he said with a bow.

Henri clapped him on the back. "Thanks to you, Sigar." The two hurried down to the water's edge.

CHAPTER 33

SAVING KATERINA

Jason placed his hand on Susan's shoulder. "Are you all right?"

Susan shook her head carefully. "I've been drugged. I've lost Katerina."

Jason handed her a cup of water. "Here, start flushing that stuff out of your system."

While Susan drank the icy cold water, Jason gently massaged the back of her neck. She felt the tension loosening.

"Thank you." Susan wriggled her shoulders. "That is really helping."

She turned to look at him. "Jason, is this more of your hospital know-how?"

He nodded and screwed up his face. "Oh, yes, tension is something I know a lot about."

They both sighed together. Then they both took a deep breath together.

"Right," Susan declared, standing and brushing down her clothes. "Let's get our stuff and get down to the boat. There's a girl that needs rescuing."

⚔ ⚔

With their few possessions gathered together, the two hurried from the camp to the riverside.

The scene had changed drastically since the last time Susan had breasted the ridge above the river. Now, all was a bustle. Captain Sigar Grimaldi's crew had caught Henri's boat and towed it back to shore. The two crews were working feverishly. They carried bales and boxes and were running from one boat to the other.

"They're off-loading our cargo." Jason shaded his eyes against the rising sun. "I guess they want to lighten the load."

The two hurried down the bank and over to their boat.

Henri stopped them at the gangplank and pulled them out of the way of the running crewmen.

"This is not a trip for children," he said.

"But—" Susan began to protest.

"But nothing," Henri interrupted. "We will be a fighting boat. Only warriors and oarsmen will accompany us." He waved his hand at the boat. "We will be traveling fast. We will be rowing with the current. The lighter the boat, the faster she will go."

Jason pushed forward. "But I can fight. Watt has been teaching me. You've watched us."

Henri nodded. "Yes, you have learned a lot. Given another year or so, you would make a good foot soldier." Then he shook his head. "This is river fighting, between boats. We have to be very sudden and very effective to ensure they don't kill their prisoner."

Susan gasped. She hadn't thought of that possibility.

She pulled back and left Henri and Jason to talk. She had to think of something to rescue Katerina. She squatted down, out of the way of the hurrying river men.

Squatting caused the crystal in her pocket to dig into her thigh. "Hmmm."

She jumped up and moved over to where the two were talking. She arrived in time to hear Henri telling Jason that he had made arrangements for them to travel with Captain Grimaldi and their cargo. They would all meet farther up the river.

"But, I can...we can help." Jason was still protesting.

"That's OK, Jason." Susan pulled on his arm. She looked to Henri. "We know that what you have to do is hard, and we wish you every success. We will wait here for you. Peter will like to have us near." She bowed to Henri.

To her surprise, Henri bowed to her. "Your time-ly alarm has given us a huge advantage," he said. He leaned forward. "I know that you are Lady Katerina's true friends," he whispered. Then he thumped his right hand over his heart, clicked his heels, and hur-ried up the gangway.

The Grimaldi crew pushed the boat out into the river.

Jason yanked his arm away from Susan. He was angry. "What did you say that for?" he demanded. "We should be on that boat, helping with the rescue."

Susan grabbed his collar and pulled his face down close to hers. "My crystal," she said, "seems to think otherwise."

Jason straightened. He shook himself. "Um, for-got about the crystal," he said.

Susan smiled. She waved her hand toward the pushing crewmen. "You want to help," she said. "Help push the boat out. I'm going to explain to nice Captain Grimaldi that we will be waiting here, for our boat's return."

CHAPTER 34

CRYSTAL, CRYSTAL

Susan and Jason waved until the boat passed around the curve downriver. With the current and lightened load, the boat skimmed over the water.

Susan nodded. "They'll catch them pretty quickly, I think." She tugged Jason's arm. "We need to hurry."

Susan led the way along the forest path until they were hidden from the encampment. She found a convenient log, scraped away some of the damp moss, and seated herself comfortably. She looked up at Jason. He was pacing nervously, jumping from foot to foot. His hands roved from the sword at his hip to the knife in his belt. His face showed nothing but worry.

Eventually he stopped pacing and fronted on Susan. "We should be on that boat." He thunked his closed fist into his other hand for emphasis.

Susan nodded. She felt calm now. Calm and sure. "Do you want to be on the boat, or do you want to rescue Katerina without bloodshed?"

Jason gaped. He spun around once, running his hands through his hair. Then he plopped to the ground at Susan's feet. "You're right." He seemed lost for words.

Finally.

"How?"

Susan showed him her crystal, nestled in the palm of her hand. "It's something I haven't tried before, but I think it will work."

"What, what!"

"I have to do an experiment first."

Jason jumped to his feet. "OK, do, do."

Susan stood, too. "I need you to run into the forest for a count of two hundred." She shook her head. "Not along the path. We've been along the path. I need you to go among the trees and hide. Somewhere I can't see you."

"Are you sure this is necessary?" Jason asked.

Susan nodded. "I want to rescue Katerina as much as you do. I'm sure that's what I'm here to do." She clicked her fingers. "What's that expression? Something about going off half-cocked.

Whatever that means. Dad uses it." Susan pointed to the forest. "This experiment will be us going off full-cocked."

"OK, OK." Jason waved his arm at her and pelted into the bushes beside the path.

Susan began to count. "One caribou, two caribou…"

At two hundred caribou, Susan didn't begin looking for Jason. Instead she peered deep into her crystal. It sparkled in her palm. She formed a picture in her mind of Jason. Not just the way he looked and dressed but also the essence of him that she knew. His courage, his determination, his impatience, and his loyalty. All these aspects went into her understanding of Jasonness.

"Crystal," she ordered. "I want to go to Jason."

She landed on top of him.

"Ouch." Jason sprawled on the ground, his head stuck under a bush. Susan climbed to her feet, laughing. The relief she felt at her success made her laugh—not the fact that she'd landed right on top of Jason. *After all, I landed on top of my bed when I pictured my bedroom.* That started her laughing again. She could see success. *Crystal to the rescue.* More laughing.

"I'm glad you think it's funny," Jason grumped. "I'm wearing a bush, and it's got prickles, I think."

Susan reached down and hauled him to his feet.

"How did you do that? I didn't see or hear you coming, but there you were." Jason dusted himself off.

Instead of answering, Susan grabbed his arm and thought about the log she had been sitting on. Colors smearing and the sounds of the birds and trees melding into one sound came, and they were both back standing by the log.

Jason shook his head to clear it. "I don't think I'll ever get used to popping around like that," he said.

"Well, we're going to be doing a lot more of it. That's how I found you. I formed a picture of you in my mind and told the crystal to take me to you, and it did."

Jason rubbed his head. "Maybe you could ask the crystal to land you in front of the person rather than on top next time."

Susan laughed. "Yes, good thought."

"Here's another thought," Jason added. "Once we arrive next to Katerina, what do we do then?"

Susan sat on the log again. "I haven't plotted it all out yet. I needed to know that I could travel to a person rather than just a place."

Jason sat next to her. "OK, time to put our plotting caps on. We need to hurry if we're going to rescue Katerina and get her back to Henri before there's a battle and"—Jason held up one finger—"without getting burned as witches along the way."

Susan nodded in agreement. The two stood and walked along the path, retracing their steps from the day before. There was a lot to work out to make the rescue, get Katerina back to Henri, and remain undetected as the rescuers.

"I guess Katerina will have to know something." Susan sighed.

Jason shrugged. "Well, she already thinks we're different and mysterious. What's a bit more?"

They walked on.

CHAPTER 35
THE PLAN

They executed the first part of their plan by returning to the encampment. They made sure everyone saw them.

They ate a huge breakfast. So much had happened already this day that Susan was astounded to find breakfast on the table. Boiled eggs on fresh, crusty bread—there was ham as well. They both ate as much as they could, even though their stomachs roiled with excitement over their plans for the rest of the day. They wrapped extra food in cloth and carried that with them. Pears, grapes, more bread. As they stood from the table, Susan grabbed a wedge of cheese. *That's always good to keep us going.*

They reported to Captain Grimaldi. "We're going to watch from the cliff tops for the return of our boat," Susan told him.

He nodded in acknowledgment and patted their shoulders for comfort. Susan gave him a hug—she just felt like it. He was kind and helpful. He seemed surprised but pleased and gave a low chuckle.

"We'll watch for your return," he said and added, "Stay safe."

The pair gripped hands and hurried along the path into the forest.

For the next part of their plan, they needed to determine exactly where the boat carrying Katerina was. Susan used the crystal to jump them to the camp they had used the night before last. This was more a river resort than a camp. They arrived in the line of trees close to the river.

"Thank goodness I went for a walk after supper," Susan said.

Jason agreed. "Seems like a good habit for you to continue."

They ran down to the riverbank. An old man was fishing there. He seemed to be dozing more than catching fish, though.

"Excuse me, sir." Susan nudged him with her foot. "Have you seen a boat hurrying down the river?"

The man rolled over, grumpy. "You woke me up," he exclaimed.

Jason tapped his foot and frowned down at the man.

Susan stepped in with a more soothing tone. "We're looking for a boat. It will be rowing with the current. Going fast. Have you seen it, good sir?"

The man scratched his head. "Yep, I saw it. Don't know why they'd be rowing when the current was carrying them along. Stupid, if you ask me." He pulled on his fishing line. "No explaining some folks," he added.

Jason couldn't wait any longer. "Another boat, did you see another boat chasing the first one?"

The man shrugged. "Must've dozed off. Saw nothing after that." He looked the two up and down. "Until you two came along, disturbing an honest man's rest."

"Thank you, sir." Susan pulled Jason away.

"Young whippersnappers, racing their boats along this river. Pile up, they will. You see if I'm not right." Susan heard the man muttering to himself as they moved back into the tree line.

"On to the next." Susan sighed. This could get tricky. Finding the boats' positions seemed to be the hardest part of their quest.

Working backward, they touched each camp along the river.

At the second camp they tried, people had seen the Derrin boat and Henri's boat following along about an hour later, so they moved along to the next camp.

Here they found people who had seen the Derrin boat but not Henri's.

"I think Henri will pass here soon, though," Jason said.

"I think you're right. Henri seems to be gaining."

The two sat with their feet in the water for a moment.

"OK, so if we move two more on we should be far enough ahead for our plan to work." Jason was ready to go.

Susan nodded. "I think you're right," she said. "That should work as long as nothing goes wrong. Just let me think for a moment. What was that camp like?"

Jason piped up. "Remember, it's the camp where I first landed my sword on Watt's arm."

Susan laughed. "Yes, and Katerina gave you a flower in congratulations."

Jason nodded. "And everyone wondered why the boy called Peter was giving me flowers."

The two chuckled.

Susan chucked his arm. "And they had a donkey there. And it kicked in the side of the sty, and the pig got out, and everyone chased it all over the place."

"Yep, there. Should put us far enough ahead."

Susan grinned. "I went for a walk there, too. I know the perfect spot for us to take Katerina."

They both stood. It was hard to get their shoes on over their wet feet.

"Who was it that always said that you should carry a towel?" Jason tugged at his runner.

"Wasn't it that hitchhiker guy?" Susan dried her foot down her pant leg. "You know, the one on British television."

"Yeah, that one. Didn't he have a saying or something?"

Susan started to laugh. "Don't panic."

Jason laughed too. "Seems appropriate."

They faced each other.

Susan held tight to the crystal. "I think it might be better if we stand back to back," she said. "Then we will be able to see in both directions."

Jason nodded and, all solemn, moved behind her.

Susan concentrated. Katerina. Long black hair... nope, short black hair now. Brave. All this danger she was in was to protect her cousin. A strong family loyalty. Good, solid friends. A sense of adventure.

Flashing eyes. Haughty expression. Slim figure. Yes, that was Katerina.

"Make sure we're touching," she called to Jason.

"Crystal, take me to stand beside Katerina," she ordered.

CHAPTER 36
KATERINA

Susan and Jason had only an instant to assess the situation when they arrived at Katerina's side. Her hands were tied behind her back. She was sitting on a coil of rope, somewhere enclosed on the boat. Drust was sitting opposite her. He had a spoon in one hand and a metal pannikin half-full of porridge in the other. He seemed to be trying to feed Katerina. He had pap splattered on his face and clothes, so it looked as though Katerina didn't want to be fed.

When they arrived on the scene, Drust jumped to his feet, mouth open. Jason grabbed the metal pannikin out of his hand and whacked him across the side of the head with it. Drust fell to the floor without a sound.

"What?" Katerina's eyes opened wide. "Where did—"

Susan put her fingers to her lips. They had no time to linger. Someone could have heard Drust fall.

"Grab him?" Jason asked.

Susan nodded. "Could be useful."

Jason hauled Drust into his arms. Susan grabbed Katerina's arm. "Untie me," Katerina demanded.

"Later." Susan shook her head and thought hard. The sty with the kicked-in side. No, no, the spot in the clearing by the river. Yes, she had it. Jason leaned against her side, his arms full of Drust.

Susan formed the picture of where she wanted to go. She thought the command to her crystal—and they went.

CHAPTER 37
THE PLAN UNFOLDS

They arrived exactly where Susan wished. Instantly there was an argument.

Katerina kicked out at Drust lying on the ground where Jason had dropped him, but all her attention was riveted on Susan. "What just happened?" she yelled. "I'm somewhere else. What have you done to me?"

Susan harrumphed and put her hands to her hips. "We've just rescued you," she said as calmly as she could. "It would be a good idea to keep quiet. We don't want to attract too much attention at the moment."

Jason moved behind her and began to pick at the knots holding the rope around her wrists.

Katerina drew herself up and tried to look down her nose. In her best "lady" voice she said, "Explain."

Susan matched her. "Sit," she said and waved to a nearby fallen log.

Drust stirred his shoulders and groaned. Jason hit him with the haft end of his knife.

"Why didn't you use your sword on Drust?" Katerina asked. She massaged her wrists as she spoke.

Jason grimaced. "Swords make holes and blood leaks out. I leave a bump." He waved to Drust now lying quietly. "Now he's got two bumps but still no leaks."

Susan sniggered. Katerina glared at her for a moment, and then she, too, had to grin. Jason moved to sit cross-legged on the ground by the log. "Better hurry," he said. "That boat will be along any minute now."

Susan nodded. She took a deep breath and faced Katerina.

She opened her hand to expose the crystal.

"This is the Crystal of the North," she said.

Katerina screwed up her nose. "What is?"

"Huh." Old problem. Susan took her crystal so for granted that she forgot that most people could not see it. She remembered that Judy had almost been poked in the nose and not noticed the crystal. She had introduced Jason to it when they first began this adventure and now she needed Katerina to meet the Crystal of the North. Her crystal.

Susan pointed to it and described it. She told of its qualities and about her responsibility to help people.

Katerina squinted at the point where Susan's finger touched the crystal, and gradually, her eyes opened wide, and she stared with wonder at Susan's palm. The crystal slowly took shape and became real to her.

"This is a great magic," Katerina murmured. She reached out her finger and gently touched the crystal. Lights danced within the surface, and she gasped and tucked her finger into her armpit.

Susan laughed. "The crystal likes you," she said to reassure Katerina.

Jason cleared his throat. "Don't you think we need to finish the plan?"

Susan jumped up. "You're right," she said. "You explain the next part, and I'll get to it."

Jason nodded.

Susan felt the weight of her bag against her hip. "Oops, I almost forgot." She pulled out Katerina's blue cloak. "This will be distinctive enough for them to notice you," she said.

Katerina snuggled the soft wool to her face. She breathed deep into the folds.

Susan smiled when she saw the soft look that came over Katerina's face. Then she formed a picture of Henri's boat. She pictured the small space where they had sheltered from the wind. The space hidden from most of the crew. The crystal took her there.

Susan sank down as low as she could. She took a deep breath and peeped over the little wooden partition to see what was happening.

The boat moved rapidly along the river. Susan could see the trees on the bank from where she hid and could judge from that how fast the boat was moving. Most of the men had stripped away their tunics and even their shirts. They rowed.

Now she needed to find Watt. On his own. Susan watched.

Henri came into view, walking between the two lines of rowers. "Change," he called. The rowers shipped their oars and another group of men rushed out and swapped places with them. In moments the fresh rowers were pulling along the river again.

Watt gave up his oar and slumped against the boat's railing. He panted. His arms hung limp over the side of the boat.

After a brief rest, Watt moved through the resting rowers. He came up to the water butt, which stood close to Susan's hiding place. This was her chance.

"Psst." Susan put up her hand and beckoned with her finger.

Watt slurped water from the dipping ladle. He sighed.

"Psst. Psst." Susan waved her hand more urgently.

Watt ladled water over his head. He stretched out his arms to ease the muscles along his back.

"Watt, over here." That got his attention.

He slipped into Susan's hiding place and slumped to the floor.

"What—" He opened his mouth to speak.

Susan laid her finger on his lips. She shook her head. "No time," she whispered. "Watch the bank. Watch for Katerina. She is near the forest just past the next camp. Make sure the boat stops for her."

Watt reached his hand out to her. "How—"

Susan shook her head. "Later," she whispered. She made shooing motions with her hands.

Watt rose to his feet with a groan.

"Watch," Susan told him.

He nodded.

⟞⟝ ⟞⟝

Susan returned to Jason. He was the easiest for her to visualize.

They were on the riverbank. Katerina and Jason stood right at the water's edge. A shallow area led down into the water. It was like a small beach.

They both jumped when Susan popped into existence beside them.

Katerina squeaked. "You startled me." She frowned.

Jason chuckled. "At least she didn't land on your head."

"Where's Drust?" Susan looked around.

Jason waved up the beach. Drust sat lashed to a tree. "We used our belts and the rope from Katerina's wrists," he said.

Katerina came up to Susan and gave her a hug. "You rescued me," she said. "You are a powerful person." She shook her head. "I never thought I would be privileged to meet a wielder of true magic." She bowed very low. "I am forever in your debt. Frederick is forever in your debt." She threw her arms wide. "You will be honored in his court above all others."

Susan ran her shoe through the sand at her feet. "Really, that's not what I want."

Katerina waved her arm. "Castles, lands, peasants all—"

Jason interrupted. "The boat just rounded the bend."

Susan shook herself. "Right." She turned to Katerina. "You rescued yourself. Remember, this has to be our secret. Nobody should know what we can do."

Jason pulled Susan into the trees. They crouched down to watch.

CHAPTER 38

A VERY PRIVATE CONVERSATION

Katerina waded into the water. She removed her cloak and waved it in the air.

Susan heard Watt's yell from the boat. "Look, look, on the bank." She could see Watt jumping and pointing, just a little figure on the boat.

"That looks like Peter's blue cloak." Watt pulled Henri to the side to have a look.

Henri gave a brief glance. "Ship oars," he roared. The big boat slowed and turned into the beach. Soon the keel ground into the sand, and Katerina rushed over to stand at the bow. Watt and Henri leaped out and ran to her.

Susan could see faces all along the side, peering in wonder to see their Peter standing free on the beach.

From their hiding place, Susan and Jason watched the story unfold as Katerina told it to Henri and Watt. Susan saw her raise the pannikin and show how she bonked Drust on the head. Henri asked her a question. She shrugged. And shrugged again and again.

"Probably asking how she escaped the boat and got out here to the riverside," Jason whispered.

Susan nodded. "There are holes in the story, aren't there?"

Katerina gestured toward Drust. Watt and Henri turned toward the tree where he sprawled, trussed up.

They stalked over and stood glowering down.

Jason tugged on Susan's arm and together they crept through the trees toward the place where the trio had gathered around Drust.

They snuggled down behind a bush just in time to hear Drust say, "Ask her about the other two."

Henri slapped Drust's face, hard. "Peter told us of your cowardly acts, traitor." Henri emphasized the name Peter, but obviously Drust had seen through Katerina's disguise.

Drust shook his head. "Ask him about the other two," he sneered.

Katerina nudged him with her foot. "You're tied to a tree. We're armed. You're not. Silence is your best hope of a comfortable future."

But Watt wore a thoughtful look. He turned to Katerina. "Yes, Peter, I think you do need to tell us about the other two."

Katerina kicked Drust hard in the leg. "We should have gagged you."

Henri raised his eyebrows. "We?"

Susan sighed. She moved just a little, so that Katerina would see her. She beckoned.

Katerina nodded slightly. She looked back at the boat with all the watching faces. "Leave him here," she said, pointing to Drust. "This is going to be a very private conversation."

Katerina marched into the forest along a path. Watt hurried to follow. Henri looked around, whipped off his neck scarf, and used it to gag Drust.

Then he hurried into the forest after Katerina and Watt.

Susan and Jason stayed in their place a moment longer to ensure that all was secure on the beach and no one was following. Then Susan nudged Jason's shoulder, and they hurried to join the others.

By the time Susan and Jason joined the group, they were sitting comfortably in a circle with their backs against trees and a fallen log.

"Ah, the two." Henri greeted them as they joined the group. He waved his hand around the clearing. "Please, join us in our new council chamber."

Susan and Jason sat.

Henri continued. "Katerina has informed us that it is not important for us to know how you managed her rescue." He bowed his head in her direction. "Or

224

how she and Drust arrived on the beach so we could find her."

Katerina interrupted. "What is important is working out how to get me to Lady Beatrice as quickly as possible. Frederick's life hangs on my information getting to him."

Henri cut in. "It's also important for us to decide what to do about the boat that kidnapped you. They will find that you and Drust are gone. Will they continue to Cologne, or will they double back along the river, searching for you?"

"It will appear to them that we disappeared by magic, from their midst." Katerina spread her hands. "I think they will hurry on to Cologne to tell their masters that I am traveling as a boy and that I was on the river."

Susan had a question. "Will they know for certain that the boy Peter is Lady Katerina, or do you think they were just guessing?"

Katerina nodded. "That's a good point. They just knew that Sir Gustaff and family were looking for Lady Katerina."

"The Derrin family wouldn't have known that you were presumed dead in a dungeon fire, either. They were traveling downriver when we met in that encampment." Watt rubbed the muscles in his arms as he spoke.

Henri quirked his brows. "Not used to rowing?"

"Not as hard as that," Watt agreed.

Katerina cleared her throat. "Now we need to decide how we get to Lake Konstanz."

Henri stretched out. "It will take them another day of hard rowing to get to Cologne. Maybe another day to get a hearing with the right people. Maybe another day to send out people along the river and along the roads to try to catch up." He held out his left hand. "If we go on along the river, we will be as slow as we were before. The current is still strong. We will get there, but it will be a long journey, and we will be easily found by any boat looking for us."

Henri put out his right hand. "We are about two days south of Mainz at the moment. From here the river veers to the west. But if we travel overland from here to the lake we will shorten our journey by several days. With a small, well-armed group, well mounted and riding hard, we should be able to reach Lake Konstanz more quickly and with less problems. We will be at least four days ahead of any group setting out from Cologne in pursuit."

He weighed his two hands up and down. "Both will work. The road will be quicker, and there will be more than one route we can take, which will add to the confusion."

"Pilgrims. We can hide with the children again," Susan suggested.

Three people shook their heads. "They'll be everywhere, I agree, but that's way too slow," Henri said.

"Not everyone treats the pilgrims kindly. They are preyed upon," Watt added.

"Boys delivering horses," Jason blurted out.

Watt agreed. "It works," he said. "Not as conspicuous as soldiers, and they can be moving fast. That's what we did before."

Henri thought about it. "It is better than as soldiers. There's always livestock being moved along the roads. We won't have to find armor for the men who are going with you, either. That will lighten the horses' load." He nodded decisively. "That's going to be the best."

Katerina stood. She made motions to straighten down her dress. "Old habits." She shook her head. "It is sometimes hard to remember who and what I am. Katerina, Peter, it gets confusing."

Henri stood, too. "You do well." He thumped his chest. "I can't imagine trying to behave as a woman."

The other three looked at him. Jason shook his head. "Can't see it."

"Huh," was all the response Henri made. He was all business now. "I'll take Drust with me on the boat. We will try to behave as though you are still on board. That will add some confusion." He turned to Watt. "You go into the encampment, see how many horses you can get. Good ones, mind. Enough for each person and a couple of spares for supplies." Henri pointed to Susan and Jason. "You two, stay hidden. I don't want to explain to others how you got here." He threw up his hands. "I don't know how you got here."

Katerina moved to stand beside Susan. "I'll stay with them."

Henri nodded. "Then I'm off to see which of my rowers can ride a horse. They're all good fighters."

Susan looked at the faces around her. *It should be time for one of those football cheers you see on television.*

Henri walked to Watt. He clasped his arm, and Watt clasped his. "Godspeed," he said, and they shook.

So that's how it's done here. Susan was ready when Henri approached her and she clasped his arm with a will.

Watt and Henri rushed off to fulfil their parts of the plan.

Susan slumped to the ground. "I'm so tired all of a sudden," she said.

Jason nodded. "Well, you've been jumping us around all over the place, so I'm not surprised. The energy to do that must come from you." He sat down beside her. "Try to sleep," he suggested. "I'll be here to watch."

CHAPTER 39
THEY RIDE

"Eric, Eric." Susan opened her eyes. Jason gently shook her shoulder. "You've slept as long as possible," he told her. "We're almost ready to move."

Susan sat up and rubbed her eyes. The quiet forest clearing was now all bustle and hurry.

Men and horses moved through the scene. Some men sat on the logs, gnawing on what looked to Susan like chicken drumsticks. They smelled like chicken, too. Her stomach rumbled.

Jason chuckled. "Don't worry. I saved you some." He held out a trencher to her. Chicken juice had seeped through the bread. Susan took a deep breath. It smelled wonderful. Sautéed onions, just the way her mum made them, lay on the bread under the chicken. She took her first bite of chicken. Wonderful.

Jason brought her up to date while she chewed. "You were sound asleep. You didn't even stir when Watt arrived with about fifteen horses. They were clomping around all over the place, but you didn't stir."

Susan looked around; she spotted eight horses. Big, powerful-looking animals, already saddled and standing quietly, cropping at the grass beside the pathway.

"Henri picked out the best and took the rest back," Jason explained. "We're going to be traveling with three men from the boat."

One of the men sitting on the log, Serrill, looked up and waved his chicken leg at her. He smiled.

I guess he can hear what we're saying. Susan pulled up some onions and popped them in her mouth. *Delicious. Everything tastes better when you're hungry.*

Katerina joined them where they sat. She handed Susan a cup. "Here's apple juice, Eric," she said.

"Thanks K—Peter." Susan just caught herself. *I need to wake up.*

The three looked up at the sound of horses galloping along the path. Watt rode into the clearing, closely followed by Henri.

"They just returned the horses we didn't want," Jason explained. "Oh, and Henri is coming with us."

"Can't let you youngsters have all the fun." Henri walked over, rubbing his hands together. His horse's reins were looped over his arm, and he wore a big grin. "I don't get to travel away from the river much."

Susan found herself sitting almost under the horse's hooves. It was time to move. She stood and stretched. There were a lot of kinks to get out. Watt brought over a horse for her.

"What are you going to call this one?" he asked as he handed her the reins.

Big and brown, the horse tossed its head at her. There was a blaze of white down its nose, and when she looked, she saw that the horse had two white hooves while the back two were brown.

Watt slipped her an apple. "He can already smell the juice on your breath. Make friends," he said and walked off to help with the other horses.

After feeding her horse, Susan moved along and saw that her bag was already firmly tied behind her saddle. Susan chuckled at the little wooden arm-chair-like saddle. She felt the cushioning. *It will never be enough.* She sighed. Jason gave her a leg up.

"Well, off we go, I guess," he said and moved over to his own mount.

"Have you thought of a name for yours yet?" Susan asked as Jason wrestled with his horse. It cavorted away from him as he tried to get his foot into the stirrup.

"Not yet," Jason answered, hopping around with one foot in the stirrup, "but I'm thinking about Grinch." He grabbed the saddle and hauled himself up. "That's better." He sighed, settling himself. Then his face lit up. "Silver, I'm going to call him Silver."

Susan laughed. "But he's brown."

Jason nodded. "I know, but I've always wanted to say"—he took a deep breath—"hi-ho, Silver."

Susan couldn't help it. It was just too silly. She just doubled over, laughing. All the tension drained out of her body. With all the danger; the dashing about; saving Katerina over and over again; the crystal and learning to do new things with it; being so far from home; all that had built up inside her, and now she laughed it all away. Jason. *How lucky I am to have Jason along on this adventure,* she realized.

Katerina brought her horse up alongside Susan. "Can we all share the joke?"

Susan shook her head. "I don't think it will translate," she said. Katerina looked disappointed. Susan thought about it. "Jason is going to call his horse Silver."

"But it's brown," Katerina said with a frown.

"Exactly," Susan replied.

Katerina looked at her sideways. "Sometimes I don't understand you at all, Eric," she said and moved her horse over to stand beside Henri. Susan nudged her horse to follow.

They were soon all grouped around Henri. Susan knew Serrill but didn't know the names of the other two boatmen.

One of them noticed her looking. "Wulfric. At your service." He bowed his head in her direction and clapped his hand to the sword at his side.

"Meles. At your service also." The third boatman's grin broadened. "But I don't like to cook," he added.

Susan grinned in acknowledgment. She surveyed the group. *Eight people, ten horses,* she thought. *Will we be inconspicuous?*

Henri clapped his hands. "We are going hard and fast," he told them. "It's many days' ride, but we must keep ahead of our enemies. The story is that we are just lads. We are delivering horses for the Margrave of Bavaria. Remember that name. It's important. The Margrave of Bavaria. We must get them there as quickly as possible, or we will not be paid."

All nodded.

Henri gave the signal and turned his horse to lead the party out of the forest along the path.

When they reached the beach, Susan saw that the boat had already left and Drust was no longer tied to the tree. *I hope Jason and Katerina got their belts back.*

They soon reached the path that led to the encampment, and they followed it to the road. *More like a slightly wider path.* Susan braced herself. Henri set the pace, and the horses seemed pleased to stretch out into an easy gallop.

Susan sighed. Her thigh and leg muscles were not pleased.

Her mount settled in next to Katerina's, and Jason and Watt rode behind them. *I'm going to call this horse Nanaimo,* she decided. *Just a touch of home.*

They rode on.

CHAPTER 40

ON THE ROAD AGAIN

July was high summer in the Holy Roman Empire. The days were long and hot. Henri made that first day's ride fairly short. They all needed to settle in for what was ahead.

There was an encampment close to the road where they stopped.

"This is an easy day," Henri warned them. "Get your gear sorted and comfortable because tomorrow we will be riding all the long day." He turned to Meles. "You can cook."

Everyone chuckled. Meles sighed and shrugged.

"I'll cook." Wulfric laughed. "I want to be able to eat it. Meles, you gather some wood for the fire."

And so the rhythm of the following days was settled. They rode on. And on.

━◆ ◆━

Before dawn on the third day Henri shook the tent. "Get up. Come on. We need to move."

Susan sat up sighing. Katerina groaned and pulled her blanket over her head.

Outside the tent Susan found a busy scene. Serrill had the fire going. Watt and Meles had four horses saddled and were working on the others.

Only three days into this wild ride, and Susan felt as though she had never done anything else.

Susan sighed and took a deep breath. She scratched across the back of her neck. She felt dusty. *What I wouldn't give for a hot shower.* She ran her fingers through her hair. *With lavender shampoo.* The thought made her sigh.

All day they alternated the horses between an easy gallop and a stretch of walking. A few times the road led over hills, and Watt suggested everyone dismount and lead the horses.

"We've a long way to go," he explained. "The health of the horses is crucial to us right now."

Susan liked the walking. It helped her stretch her legs. Walking used a different set of muscles, and it felt good. There was less dust when they walked, too.

That was a decided bonus. She tried to stay positive, but she was not enjoying this wild ride across the countryside.

She looked around her, taking in all the scenery as they passed: the fields, the forests, the little farms, and the small villages. All would look so different if she visited them in her time.

In several places, other roads joined the one they were traveling. In the early afternoon, they arrived at a crossroads, and from then on, the road was busy with merchants and pilgrim children.

"We've joined the main road from Cologne now," Henri informed them when they dismounted to walk the horses again. And so they walked.

Katerina gasped. Susan looked up to see Katerina ducking her head and swinging around to the opposite side of her horse. Susan ducked around Nanaimo and came up beside Katerina. "What is it?" she asked. "What's wrong?"

Katerina peeped over the back of her horse. Susan sneaked a peek, too. "Those pilgrims." Katerina pointed. "I recognized one. We gave him the food to give to Grefin on the road before Cologne."

Susan looked hard. She was so used to sharing the road with gaggles of children, all plodding along.

"You're right," she said. "I guess they've left Cologne. Nicholas has them all walking to Jerusalem now." Susan shook her head at the sight.

"We mustn't be recognized. We must ride and get away." She mounted her horse and rode forward to speak to Henri and Watt.

Susan patted Nanaimo on the nose. "You're a good horse," she whispered. "I'm riding again, it seems." Nanaimo stood for her while she climbed into the saddle. *Not too graceful but I managed,* she thought with satisfaction.

Jason rode up beside her. "Is something up?"

Susan waved at the children plodding along the side of the road.

"Katerina is worried that we might be recognized by some of the children."

"Surely the ones we know are way behind us," Jason replied. "Think how many miles we've traveled since we left them." Then he added, "I sort of hope they gave up and went home." He flapped his hands at the children. "Or something."

Susan nodded. She understood how he felt.

"But," she reminded him. "We hopped back at least four days of our rowing along the river. They could be on this part of the road." She turned her head resolutely forward and kicked Nanaimo into a trot. Jason followed her closely.

Their group, all mounted now, broke into an easy gallop and soon outdistanced that particular group of children. But there were others. All along that stretch of road, they passed clumps of children struggling along. Some singing and happy and other just doggedly putting one foot in front of the other.

⊫⊹ ⊹⊨

Henri called a halt when they reached an open clearing beside the road. It was obviously a common stopping place along the way as Susan could see where fire pits were dug and marked with stones. Some logs had been pulled around to form seating.

Several groups already occupied areas of the clearing. Tents were set up, and a few wagons were pulled to one side and covered with tough cloth. *The owners probably sleep under there to protect their property,* Susan decided.

Henri led their group to an isolated spot near the back of the clearing. "We'll camp here," he said. "Hopefully it won't get too crowded."

Katerina agreed. "It's better that we don't have too many neighbors noticing what we do and who we are."

Susan dismounted with a sigh of relief and slumped onto one of the logs set around their fire pit. Serrill came over and gently took Nanaimo's reins from her hands. "Here, you rest," he said with a smile. "You look so tired." He sat beside her. "I'm not sure what you did back there at the river." He looked at Susan with raised eyebrows. "But you did it." He flexed his arms. "You saved me a lot of hard rowing and a boat battle at the end of it, so I'm grateful." He patted her knee and stood. "You sit. Rest. I'll look after your horse." Serrill clicked his tongue and tugged on the reins. The horse didn't move. Serrill looked down at Susan. "What did you call this horse again?"

"Nanaimo," Susan told him with a grin.

"C'mon, Nan…Nan…How do you say it?"

Susan laughed. She whacked Nanaimo on the rump. "Don't worry about it, Serrill. Nobody gets it right first try."

Jason slid onto the log beside her. "I still don't always get it right, and I lived there for over a month." He chucked Susan on the shoulder. "Really, you had to call your horse Nan…Nanaimo?"

Susan shrugged. "Touch of home," she said.

"I'm setting some snares." Jason searched in his bag. "If I can remember how it's done," he said and marched off into the trees behind their camp.

Katerina perched on the log next to Susan and stretched her legs out in front of her. "I won't be able to do this much longer." She sighed. "It will be back into long skirts, and 'ladies do this' and 'ladies do that.'" She spread her arms wide. "I feel so free out here."

Susan looked at her sideways. She was skeptical. "You'll have servants and people to cook and clean for you."

"Huh." Katerina scrubbed her boots in the dirt.

Susan continued. "And there'll be no one trying to kill you, and you won't have to sleep in a tent or eat rabbit cooked over an open fire. You'll live in a grand palace."

"Huh." Katerina dismissed that with a wave of her hand. "And then they'll find someone for me to marry, and I'll have a castle to look after. There will be squads of servants that I have to supervise, and I will need to be sure that there are enough candles made and that there is enough food for everyone. And that the maids are all behaving themselves with the soldiers. That will all be my responsibility." Katerina paused for a breath.

Susan patted her hand and chuckled. "I thought you just had to wander around, pointing at things, and they got done, and then you sat with your lady friends and embroidered shirts for your husband."

"Huh." Katerina rubbed her hands together. "Lady 'friends' will be sent to my castle. Half are spies for lords looking for power, and the others have no skills, and you're expected to teach them how to run a castle, and...and"—Katerina tapped Susan's arm for emphasis—"they're all just there for me to find them husbands."

Susan put her head on Katerina's shoulder for a moment. "I had no idea," she said. "I thought you lived a life of ease."

Katerina shook her head. "Everyone works," she said. "And what I've just told you is just how it is if I get a good husband. If I get a lout like that Sir Gustaff, then it's way more difficult, and you have to keep everything going—and you just sort of hope he'll go off to liberate Jerusalem and leave you in peace."

The two girls sat side by side on the log. Susan watched the activity as the camp took shape around her. The horses were tended. Jason walked back through the trees, holding up a rabbit. He'd obviously had success with his snare. There was a fire going, and Wulfric already had vegetables bubbling in a pot. Meles was setting up the tents in a row. Henri was off talking to some of the other campers in the clearing.

"What would your life have been like with Sir Robert?" Susan remembered the fond letter that Katerina had received way back at the beginning of the adventure.

Katerina quietly wiped a tear from the corner of her eye. "I was thinking about him, too," she said. "He would have made a fine husband for me." Her eyes looked across the camp, but her thoughts were far away. "He was fun." Katerina smiled slightly. "He and I rode all over the hills together. That's the important part. We were together. He wanted to do things with me, not just ride off with the other men."

Katerina swiped at her eyes again. "It was a hope, really, nothing more."

This was so different from the way Susan understood love and marriage.

"Why? If you loved him and he loved you, wouldn't that have been perfect?"

"He is just a small landholder. His family is not important enough to marry the cousin of the emperor of the Holy Roman Empire."

"Did you care that he wasn't important?"

Katerina shook her head. "No. But that wasn't even the worst of it."

"There's more?"

Katerina nodded and gave a little smile. "He was the sworn man of King John of England. He didn't like him, but he was his king. Robert was representing King John at the court of Otto IV when the pope excommunicated Otto. And then Frederick was elected emperor.

"Robert's situation was shaky. But he was King John's man. That's why he was at Sir Gustaff's castle. King John is Otto's uncle. He supported Otto and wanted him to be emperor again." Katerina shrugged. "Frederick could never allow me to marry an Englishman while John is king."

Susan sighed. She stood and stretched. "Politics," she said. "I'll never understand it."

Katerina sighed, too. She stood and put her arm across Susan's shoulder. "It's not the politics. It's the power."

They moved off together to spread their blankets in the tent Meles had set up for them.

CHAPTER 41

A DEATH

"Peter, Eric, the food is ready. Come and eat." Henri called them to supper.

Susan's stomach growled. So did Katerina's. They looked at each other. Their stomachs growled again. That set them both to laughing.

"Let's eat." Katerina lifted the tent flap and ushered Susan through. Susan mock bowed and stood waiting for Katerina. Arm in arm they moved to the fire.

"Maybe you could become one of my ladies," Katerina whispered as they joined the others.

Susan squeezed her hand. She didn't know what to say. It was a generous offer. She now had some insight into how bleak Katerina's life could become.

Spitted rabbit, cooked vegetables. A trencher of bread. It smelled wonderful. The two sat side by side on the log closest to the fire. Susan looked around their little camp. Eight companions sitting, eating together. It was so familiar to her now. This time.

If you don't look at the clothes and the horses in the background and that the men are wearing swords and that we're eating with our fingers off slabs of bread instead of plates it could be a picnic at home.

Wait. It's nothing like home.

So why does it feel as though it is?

Ah, it's the feeling. It's the companionship and the trust in one another while sharing food that's the same. The physical world changes over time, but people and what they care about and who they are, deep down, seems to be the same.

Susan took a swig of watered wine from her cup. She sat and just enjoyed the moment. Pictures of Jeremy and the immigrants on the ship ran through her head. Djus, caring and dutiful, striving to keep Egypt at peace pushed the Jeremy pictures aside, and now, here she was in Medieval Europe—Katerina striving to save her cousin, Watt faithfully helping in every way he could. Henri brave, resolute, and capable.

Different settings and very different people but some underlying feeling made them all valued and important to Susan. She stared off into the trees, not really seeing her surroundings but following in her mind's eye through her adventures.

Katerina laughed. "We saved you some," she said. Susan started back to the present. Watt had just returned to their fire. He bent over the pot and ladled vegetables onto his trencher. He picked up the last leg from the rabbit and gnawed at it as he came over to where they were sitting. Jason moved to sit with them as well.

"You were gone a long time," he said.

Watt nodded. He licked his fingers. "I watched," he said. "Grefin and his group of children came in late." He picked up a carrot and waved it toward the other end of the clearing. "They're over there."

Susan stood to have a look, but night had crept in. It was too dark to see detail around any of the little fires in the clearing.

"How are they?" Jason asked.

Watt shook his head. "They look worn out. They made a fire, but they didn't seem to have any food with them. Mostly they just slumped to the ground around the fire."

Susan started rummaging in her bag. "I've got some apples in here somewhere," she said. "We must get some food for them."

The other three nodded. Katerina stood and walked to the fire. She gathered up what was left of the bread and the pot with the vegetables.

"Did you see Petriona?" Jason asked.

Watt nodded. "Yes, she's still with them."

Henri joined their group. "What's happening?" he wanted to know.

Katerina explained while adding to the store of food she gathered.

Henri shook his head. "You can't be seen by anyone who might recognize you."

Katerina drew herself up. "These children hid me and protected me. I owe them," she said.

Henri nodded. "I understand. Watt can take the food to them."

Watt walked to the tent he shared with Jason and returned to the group with his blanket. "The weather is warmer." He shrugged. "I can do without." With Jason's help, he bundled the food into the blanket.

Jason picked up the pot. "I'll bring it back when it's empty," he promised.

He and Watt set off across the camp to where Grefin and the children were camped.

Susan tugged on Katerina's arm. "Come on, Peter. I want to see how they're all doing."

Katerina jumped up. Henri put a restraining hand on her arm.

"We'll be careful," Susan promised. "After all we're just a couple of lads out for a walk."

Katerina nodded. "We'll keep to the shadows."

Henri took his hand from Katerina's arm. "Take no risks," he said. "Yell if you need help."

Susan and Katerina hurried to catch up with the boys.

They moved quietly through the campers until Watt found the right fire. There were the children sprawled out on the ground. Grefin sat, slumped, with his back against a tree. Several of the children were gathered around him, and a blanket had been thrown over them. Grefin's eyes were shut, but he didn't seem to be asleep.

Watt walked over to Grefin and gently shook his shoulder. Jason moved the pot over to the fire. He set it close. Grefin started awake and jumped to his feet. The children around him whimpered and stirred. A couple stood, too.

"Shh, shhh." Watt shook his shoulder gently. "It's me, Watt. I saw you arrive." He gestured toward the fire. "We've brought you some food."

Grefin sighed. "You startled me," he exclaimed. Susan and Katerina stayed back in the shadows. Grefin took a deep breath. *He smells the food*, Susan realized.

"Ah." Grefin let out the deep breath. He clapped his hands. Children started up from where they were lying. "Our friend Watt has brought us food."

The children rose and moved toward the smell. Jason quickly broke off pieces of bread and sopped it in the juices from the vegetable pot. As quickly as he could do this, the bread was snatched from his hands and stuffed into hungry mouths.

Watt took out his knife and began cutting the apples into slices, which he passed to the children.

Grefin watched for a while. He accepted a slice of apple. "It's long since we have seen you, friend Watt." He munched on the apple. "Many miles separate the place of our last meeting and this."

Watt nodded but said nothing. He began passing out raisins, which had been at the bottom of Susan's bag.

Grefin continued. "You seem to have fared well. Are you, too, traveling to Jerusalem?"

Watt shook his head. "My duty lies elsewhere," he said.

Grefin nodded. "Well, you are certainly doing the Lord's work here. This food was greatly needed."

With the food consumed, the children gathered around Grefin where he sat with his back against the tree.

"Oh, you want a story now, do you?" Grefin laughed. The children nodded and smiled.

Katerina and Susan crept closer but made sure they stayed outside the ring of firelight. Jason and Watt sat among the children.

"Tell us about the sea," one of the children piped up.

"Yes, yes," the others agreed.

Grefin nodded and began telling the latest story.

"Nicholas said that we wouldn't have to walk all the way to Jerusalem. He told us there is a quicker way. Instead we will travel to the great sea."

"The great sea...Is there a great sea?" one of the children asked.

Grefin nodded. "Nicholas says it is so. Just over the mountains, there is a wonderful, rich plain, and that will lead us to a great city."

"Tell us about the mountains." A little boy tugged at his sleeve.

"They are high," Grefin continued. "But not too high. There are paths through them that we can follow."

An older boy piped up. "I thought he said passes, not paths."

Katerina gripped Susan's arm. Susan looked at her quickly, but Katerina shook her head. Susan saw that she was alarmed.

Grefin, meanwhile, had agreed with the older boy. "He did say passes, but I think that pass is just the name they give to paths that go through the mountains."

Several of the children nodded.

"Tell us the good bit. Tell us what will happen when we reach the sea."

Grefin smiled. "Ah, yes, that is the good bit. When we reach the sea, which laps at the feet of the city, Nicholas told us that we will all pray together. We will kneel there at the water's edge and pray."

The children sighed. "We'll pray together," they whispered.

"And, and..." Grefin smiled. He was holding on to the story's end. "And then God will open the seas for us, and we will walk through the sea path all the way to Jerusalem."

The children sighed happily and snuggled together, ready for sleep now. Katerina sprang to her feet and stalked off into the night.

Susan wasn't sure whether to follow her, but she watched Katerina heading resolutely back to their own campfire. She turned her attention back to what was happening around Grefin.

Watt and Jason stood. Jason nodded to Grefin.

"Thank you for your story," Watt said. "May fortune follow your dreams, and may you arrive safely in the Holy Land." He made a short bow to Grefin.

Grefin stood. He put his hand to Watt's shoulder. "I was sorry to hear of your friend's passing," he said with a shake of his head. "She seemed a brave soul, and we were glad to have her with us for a short time. We prayed for her and trust she is resting in heaven now."

Watt stared. "Grefin, thank you for your words. Who told you she was dead?"

Grefin rubbed his hands and moved closer to the fire. "Ah, another story," he said. Jason and Watt followed him into the firelight. Susan leaned forward on her log. She wanted to hear every word.

"Some days past," Grefin began, "we were trudging along the path, and a group of nobles passed us."

"How large?" Watt wanted to know.

Grefin shrugged. "The knights that attacked us looking for the lady were there. All dressed in black. They had an escort of soldiers." He thought a moment. "About as many as the fingers of my hand."

"How do you know it was the same knights?" Watt asked.

"I would recognize that Welf anywhere," Grefin declared with a scowl. "He hit you with his mailed fist. I would not soon forget him." Grefin straightened his tunic with a tug. "Once I recognized him, I could see that the other two were the same that had been with him that day." Grefin looked around at his sleeping charges. "They passed us. We kept walking."

Watt looked puzzled. "So who told you that the lady was dead?"

"Ah." Grefin nodded. "That night while we were resting, the kindest one rode into our camp. He brought us food and gave us money for the road.

He told us that his lady love had been burned in a dreadful fire at her palace in Cologne."

I bet they weren't mentioning that she was supposedly a boy in the dungeon at the time, Susan thought.

But Watt had more questions. He ran his hands through his hair. "But did he say why they were on this road and dressed in black?"

Grefin nodded. "Yes, he did. The poor man was so upset. I think he loved the lady dearly. He told us they were traveling to bring the terrible news to the grandmother of the lady. She lives on a lake somewhere."

Watt nodded. "Were they riding hard or slowly, these men?"

"Slowly, I think. They seemed to be stopping at every inn along the way. We heard the next day about the trouble they had caused at the next inn." Grefin shook his head. "Most of them didn't seem saddened at the lady's passing." He looked up. "I think they were just pretending to be sad." Then he grimaced. "Except for the one who visited us."

"Thank you for this news, Grefin." Watt bowed to the boy. "We hadn't heard of her death or that Sir Gustaff was on the road. This is valuable information for us." Watt reached into his belt pouch and pulled out another coin, which he gave to Grefin.

Jason fished out another coin as well. "Thank you," he said.

Jason picked up the empty vegetable pot, and the two turned and headed toward their camp.

Susan joined them as they passed her. She was so full of questions.

"Not a word," Watt muttered and strode on. Jason and Susan worked to keep pace with him.

CHAPTER 42

AN IDEA

"They're ahead of us!" Katerina stamped her foot in frustration. "I was upset enough that those poor children were going to clamber over the Alps and then expect the sea to part for them at Genoa." She kicked dust into the fire. "Now, I hear that Gustaff is on his way to Grandmother with news of my death." She slumped down onto a log. "And he's ahead of us," she said in a small voice.

Susan sat next to her and put her arm around Katerina's shoulders. "I know you're upset, but we will work this out somehow, you'll see."

Henri came stumbling out of his tent, sword in hand. "What's going on?" He looked around the camp. "Who's on watch?"

Meles moved quietly into the firelight; waved his hand to Henri, who nodded to him; and sank back into the shadows.

"Humph." Henri threw his sword back into the tent. "So what's all the fuss about then?" he wanted to know.

All in a rush and talking over one another, the four told him everything they had learned from Grefin. For the entire telling, Henri stood, head down and arms folded.

When the children finally fell silent, he looked up at them. He searched each face around the group. Finally his eyes alighted on Katerina. "Then we must get to your grandmother before they do." He spread his arms wide. "She would be devastated to hear that you were dead. She has been worried and upset that you were stuck in that Welf castle throughout this mess."

Katerina crossed her arms and glared at him. "Hmmph," she retorted. "She sent me there."

Henri nodded slowly. "They were different times."

Katerina lowered her eyes. "Yes, well…" She sank onto a log. "What will we do?"

Watt straightened his shoulders. "We will have to get there first," he declared.

Henri stroked his beard. "I agree. But we have to pass them to do that. There is no road faster than this one."

Susan piped up. "Well, where is Katerina?" She looked around. "I don't see a Katerina anywhere here. Do you?"

Watt pointed at Katerina.

Susan shook her head. "No, no, that's Peter. Everyone knows that. That's Peter, and I'm Eric."

Wulfric had joined the circle by this time, drawn from his tent by all the chatter. "Except when you forget and then you're Peter and that one is Eric."

They heard Meles chuckle from the trees. Serrill crawled sleepy-eyed from the tent.

Susan shrugged. "The point is there's nobody in this group that looks like Lady Katerina." She looked around. "Is there?"

All shook their heads. Serrill poked at the fire and threw on some more wood. "Looks as though sleeping is over for the night." He yawned.

"Oh no," Henri declared. "Sleeping is exactly what we are going to do—now. Because at first light, we're going to ride. And ride hard."

Wulfric rubbed his hands together. "We'll blow right past them." He smiled.

"Yep," Serrill agreed. "We'll probably come across them while they're still sleepy and suffering from a night of drinking. They won't even notice us."

Susan stood and stretched. "Maybe we'll pass them early in the morning before they've left their inn, and we'll never see them at all," she said.

Henri nodded sharply. "That would be the best solution." He clapped his hands. "Now, sleep," he said.

Susan helped Katerina to her feet, and the two walked to their tent.

"It will work out," Susan told Katerina. "You'll see."

Katerina stopped in her tracks and turned to Susan. "Can't you jump us there?"

Susan was surprised by the thought. She shook her head sadly. "I knew you. I could focus on you, and then the crystal took me to where you were." She drew Katerina on toward their tent. "I knew the camps because we had been there before. I don't know anything about where we're going now or any of the people there."

Katerina's shoulders slumped. "Good night," she said and slipped into the tent.

"Good night," Susan said as she joined her.

Katerina fell asleep almost instantly, but Susan had a lot to think about.

CHAPTER 43
SERRILL'S STORY

They broke camp before the sun peeped over the horizon. They were galloping along the road before most of the people in the camp had thrown back their blankets.

They rode all day, spelling the horses, walking them, leading them, and then galloping again.

At the beginning of their ride, the road was clear, and they made good time. As the day wore on, though, other merchants and travelers joined them on the road. At one point, they caught up with local farmers carrying their produce into the next little town. They led their horses through a flock of sheep. They passed handcarts and larger carts drawn by donkeys.

Travelers used the road in both directions, so often it was clogged. People would meet and stop for a chat. If the forest dipped down to the road, then they stood in the road to talk. The road was narrow, and so the carts stood with the people.

As they dismounted to skirt around yet another chatting knot of farmers, Serrill sidled up to Susan where she was leading Nanaimo. "Just be glad it hasn't been raining," he said. "We could be doing all of this over our ankles in mud."

"Huh." Wulfric lifted a small child out of harm's way and joined them. "Almost makes you wish we were bully soldiers. Then you could just start yelling and go through at a full gallop."

Susan looked up, surprised. "But don't people get hurt when they do that?"

Wulfric grinned. "Yep," he said. "That's why we don't do it."

Serrill laughed sarcastically. "Oh yes," he said. "Do you think Welfs care if someone gets hurt as long as they get where they want to go?"

Susan glanced up quickly and noted the grim expression on Serrill's face. She nodded. "When we first saw Sir Gustaff, Klaus, and Robert, they were thundering down a little road and didn't care that there were pilgrim children wandering along."

Serrill nodded sharply. "And they don't care about farmers returning tired from market day, either," he said. He mounted his horse and caught up with the others.

Wulfric turned to Susan. "Here, I'll give you a leg up," he offered.

Susan was grateful for the help. Once she was seated, she asked the question that was worrying her. "Did I say something to upset Serrill?"

Wulfric shook his head. "Don't worry about it," he assured her. "Welfs rode down his little brother when the family was returning to their farm after a market day."

Susan nodded slowly and looked ahead at Serrill's slumped shoulders.

"He tried to grab the boy, but he tripped on the roots of a tree growing close to the road." Wulfric shuddered.

"The horse rode right over the boy. They put him on the cart and took him home."

"What happened?" Susan asked.

Wulfric waved his hand. "It took Goren three days to die." He shook his head. "None of his limbs were broken, but he was broken inside. He swelled up and leaked blood. There was nothing any of us could do."

"Were you there?" Susan asked.

Wulfric nodded. "We have always been friends, Serrill and me. I dug the hole we buried Goren in. Then Serrill and I packed up what we had and traveled to join the fight against the Welfs." He paused. Then added, "I hope we do meet up with Sir Gustaff

and his lot. They have something to answer for."
Wulfric clucked his tongue and moved his horse forward to ride beside Serrill.

Susan rode on. Watt and Jason rode along behind her.

They stopped for a brief rest in one little village. It was market day, and they took the opportunity to find food for themselves and oats for the horses. Henri's horse had cast a shoe, and they had to wait while the smith fitted a new one. They sat in the shade of an oak tree that grew on the side of the little church. It was good to rest in the shade. Susan and Katerina kept hats pulled well over their faces. Just a group of lads taking horses to the Margrave of Bavaria.

Susan watched everything. It was all so different. *I said I needed to learn more history,* she thought, *but here I am living it. There is so much here that I don't understand.* She clenched her fist on her knee.

I'm learning more about my crystal, at least, she thought with a smile. That drew her thoughts to the river and the way she had used her crystal to rescue Katerina. And that led her back to Katerina's question. Could she go to a place she didn't know? The crystal had taken her to the ship without her knowing. Harsheer had pulled her to Egypt without her consent. She shook her head. But every time she had deliberately gone to a place, she had been able to picture the place or the person in her mind.

Shortly, Henri led his horse from the stable. It was stepping lightly again. Jason groaned and pulled himself to his feet. They all stood, stretched, and scratched.

They mounted and rode on.

The rest of the day passed in the same manner as the morning. In places the road was crowded. Sometimes they were able to gallop. Sometimes the road was in good repair, and in other places, it was a rutted, dusty mess. Whatever the conditions, they traveled as fast as they could.

At dusk they came into quite a large town. Henri shook his head at the idea of staying at the inn. "It wouldn't do us much good if we were stuck at the inn and found that Gustaff was also staying there, now would it?" he explained.

They moved on down the road until they found a cleared area where other travelers were camping. They made camp quickly.

Once again, Serrill took Nanaimo for grooming. Susan was so grateful. She drew a little away from the others and sat with her back against a tree. The ground was mossy and damp under her, but she didn't even notice that discomfort. Her hand was in her pocket firmly clasped around her crystal. The crystal had brought her to this time and place and dragged Jason along with her. Had she really been a help? She'd saved Katerina, she supposed, but was that all? Her mind went round and round.

"You're too quiet." Jason dropped to the ground beside her.

Susan jumped. She put her hand to her heart. "Jason, you scared me half to death," she exclaimed.

Jason poked her in the ribs. "Only half?" He turned and rested his back against the tree, too. They were shoulder to shoulder. "Anyway," he continued. "You're too quiet."

Susan nodded. "I've been thinking."

"Uh-oh." Jason nudged her.

"Katerina asked me why I don't just jump everyone to the place we're going to."

"But you've never been there."

Susan nodded. "That's what I told her." Susan pulled the crystal out and looked at it. "But I didn't know I could jump to people until the other day, and now I know that. What else don't I know?"

Jason pulled away from the tree and turned to look at her. "Didn't you tell me that you had a paper with instructions on it, and it was blank, but then you fixed that by going to ancient Egypt?"

Susan nodded and quirked a smile. "Yes, well, that didn't work out quite how I expected."

"How did it? Tell me. This looks like something you need to get off your chest."

Susan took a deep breath. "It's a longer story than I would like it to be," she warned.

CHAPTER 44

THE INSTRUCTIONS

"I had just got back from Egypt when you arrived." Susan laughed. "I'd no sooner landed on my bed than I heard Judy calling to you from the front porch."

Jason nodded. "I saw her waving from the verandah. I thought it was you."

"Huh." Susan continued, "Well, I was dressed 'Egyptian princess' still. And I had a youth lock."

Jason slapped his leg. "Oh, I remember that. You came bursting down the stairs two at a time, out of breath—come to think of it, you did look pretty panicked."

"Well, I was. I wanted you to like me, and I'd not had time to even think about what I would say to you or anything. Part of my head was still in Egypt, and

I'd just said good-bye to my best friend there. My head was spinning."

Jason reached over and ruffled her short hair. "And then Judy pulled off your hat."

"Yep." Susan finger combed her hair. "I could've killed her. She's so unthinking like that."

"Biggest silence I'd heard in ages." Jason chuckled. "We sat on the stairs, together. Right then, we were together. I felt like I'd known you all my life."

Jason sat back on his heels and looked earnestly at Susan. "You know, I've never told you this, but from that very moment and through all this running around Europe, I have always felt safe with you." He put his hand to his heart. "You, Susan Sinclair, make me feel safe."

Susan looked down and ran her fingers through the damp moss at her side. A smile crept across her face.

Jason sat back down with his back to the tree. "Now tell me about the instruction paper. No more stalling."

Susan nodded. "It was early the next morning before I got a chance to look at the paper. I was so full of hope that I was finally going to learn more about my crystal and the many ways I could use it. I spread the paper out on my bed and began to read the hieroglyphics."

"What are they?"

"Oh, that's the formal way that the ancient Egyptians wrote." Susan waved her hand. "It's how all the engravings in tombs and such are written."

"And you could read it?"

Susan nodded. "Djus taught me."

"Well, what did it say?"

"Huh, not much. It was written by a priestess of the temple of Maat. Basically it just told how a Chosen of Maat—that's me—created four crystals. The Guardians of each crystal would be called upon to help maintain the balance in the world." Susan sighed.

"Well, I already knew all that," she continued. "But down in the bottom corner, there was a little note written in the Hieratic script, saying that the crystal had been found in the Valley of the Kings and that as this was the Crystal of the North, it was being hidden in a box of jewelry that was being sent to Greece with a princess."

"Well, that wasn't much help, was it?" Jason scratched his chin.

"No, it wasn't, but it did give me a clue to what was happening with the paper."

Jason nudged her shoulder. "Spill."

Susan laughed. "Nah, maybe we should go see if supper is cooked."

Jason grabbed her arm. "Tell me," he insisted.

Susan nodded. "I was disappointed to start with, thinking that the Egyptian was all there was and that I was never going to learn how to use the crystal properly. But then one day when you were napping and I was working in the studio, I thought about what Mrs. Coleman had said. She told me there were instructions. So there must be instructions on the paper. I just hadn't figured it out yet. So I went back and looked at the paper again. It was a week after my first look. When I opened the paper again, all the hieroglyphics had faded and all the writing was now in another script, even the little note on the bottom. I looked up the script and it was now all in Greek. And the most exciting part was that there was now more little notes jotted around the paper.

"I realized that the writing on the paper is slowly coming back, but it is going through the stages. It wasn't just one instruction sheet. It was lots of little notes jotted on the paper as the different Guardians down through the ages added what they had learned."

"That's amazing." Jason just stared ahead. Then he looked down at his hands. "Sitting in my hospital bed, I used to dream of other lives I could have, but I'd never imagined anything like the reality of what has happened to you—to us. I'm so lucky to be along on this adventure."

Susan stood and stretched. "Thanks," she said. "I'm glad to have you along. This is the first time that I've got to share and I like it."

"So," Jason wanted to know, "what language was the paper in last time you looked?"

Susan laughed. "I looked it up. It's called Runes, and it was mostly used by the Celts and the Vikings. There's lots of notes now, on both sides of the paper, so once it gets to English, it's going to be really help-ful for me."

Jason looked over at her. "No, I think you will have figured out way more things that you can do before the English language appears."

A breeze wafted by. Susan sniffed. "All this talk-ing has made me hungry. Let's eat."

Jason rubbed his bottom. "Oh, good, then anoth-er day of hard riding tomorrow."

CHAPTER 45
THE RED STAG

Ａnd it was another day of hard riding.

They were up before the sun. Mist still drifted in the fields they passed. They ate breakfast in the saddle. Henri instructed the four to wear wide-brimmed hats and to keep them low over their faces. Susan was happy to do so, as the morning sun shone in their faces. As the day wore on and the way became hot and dusty, Susan was even happier to keep her hat pulled down well over her face.

They passed other travelers along the way, much as they had on other days, but they seemed to be ahead of pilgrim children. *I guess they haven't made it this far yet,* she thought.

There was little conversation as they rode. They galloped as much as they could, and even when walking the horses, they were too tired to chat.

They stopped briefly for lunch. The horses needed a spell. They rested near a stream so that the horses could drink and cool down. The riders flopped under the trees, resting in the shade.

As the food was being packed away into saddle-bags again, Henri came over to where Katerina and Susan were sitting.

"We have ridden hard today," he said. "We have seen no sign of Gustaff and his group. Is it possible that the pilgrim boy was mistaken?"

Susan didn't even have to think about it. "No," she said. "Grefin wouldn't mix up Sir Gustaff with another knight. And," she added, "he had too much detail about the fire and everything."

Katerina looked over her shoulder. "They're out here somewhere," she fretted.

"Well, I think, then, they must have taken the other road." He waved his hand toward the north. "It's longer but easier to travel. I think they will have gone that way." Henri turned to Watt, who had joined the group. "Didn't the pilgrim boy say that they were just idling along?"

Watt nodded. "He said he thought they were partying their way along—even though they were dressed in black."

Henri rubbed his hands together. "Then I think they've gone the slow, easy way. Tonight I think we should stop at the inn ahead. I have stayed there before. The horses will get some extra care and good feed, and we can have a good meal and a solid sleep. We'll be ready then to push on faster tomorrow."

Katerina looked worried. "Are you sure that's a good idea?"

"We all need the rest," Henri said over his shoulder as he walked over to where his horse was standing.

With a sigh, Susan mounted Nanaimo. "Oats tonight for you," she said, stroking his neck encouragingly.

And they rode on.

⟾⟽

The afternoon passed much the same as the morning. Galloping, walking, walking, galloping. The only difference for Susan was the thought of an inn at the end of the day. *Maybe I can get them to bring me some hot water, and I can have a wash. I could even wash my hair.* Susan sighed with pleasure at the thought.

As the sun was sinking behind them, they crested a hill. The road before them wound down into a shallow valley. Susan could see the roof of a large structure nestled beside a stream. Only the roof was visible as the place was surrounded by groups of shady trees. The road they were following led right past the place.

"The inn." Susan sighed and shifted in her saddle. "Is that the inn?"

Henri turned and smiled.

The mood lightened in the tired group. They set their horses at a brisk walk down the hillside and toward that peaceful-looking place.

As they drew nearer, Susan saw that a wall surrounded the inn itself. It looked to be formed from sticks woven together and then covered with mud. A sign waved in the wind, showing a red stag standing in a green field. A double gate stood open, and they entered into a large cobblestoned courtyard. The inn itself stood in front of them as they came through the gate. Two stories high, it showed lots of windows overlooking the entrance. Some windows were already glowing with candlelight. To the right as they entered, Susan noticed what looked like a dairy. Yes, she heard cows. She sniffed. Yes, she smelled cows. To the left stood the stables. Henri led their group toward the front door of the inn, which stood open. The horses' hooves clattered on the cobblestones.

It was obvious that they were not the only group staying at the Red Stag that night. As they drew near the door, Susan saw stable hands leading another group of horses off in the direction of the stables. Susan counted ten horses in the group and noticed that some had lavish harnesses. As one horse walked past her, she heard the faint jingle of little pieces of silver, which were fastened to the harness.

That's when Katerina grunted. Susan turned quickly to see what had startled her, but Katerina had already turned her horse and was kicking it into action. Out the gate Katerina galloped. Then she turned and sped off up the road.

Henri groaned. "Wulfric, Meles, Peter's horse has bolted. Go and get him back." The two turned to leave.

"No," Susan exclaimed, "Peter's horses don't bolt. He did that on purpose. I think we all need to leave."

Henri sighed. Jason looked longingly at the welcoming inn door. Serrill scratched his chin and smiled. Watt reluctantly turned his horse toward the gate. Susan beat him to it. She was off, racing after Katerina.

The others will follow.

CHAPTER 46
THE LADY BEATRICE

Susan soon passed Wulfric and Meles, but once they saw her move ahead, they hurried to catch up, and the three raced on after Katerina, who was still in the lead.

Finally, Katerina slowed. Susan, Wulfric, and Meles caught up to her. Katerina nodded to acknowledge their presence, but she said nothing. They walked the horses. A little farther ahead, they came to one of the usual camping sites along the road. A few groups were already camped, but Katerina walked her horse toward the back, close to the trees bordering the site. There they found a fire ring. As soon as she reached this area, Katerina dismounted and stood with her head buried in the heaving side of her horse. She ran her hand tenderly along its neck.

"Well, at least it's not raining," Meles grumped as he dismounted and stretched.

Susan dismounted. She patted Nanaimo. The horse had worked hard all day, and that last run seemed to have left the horse exhausted. Nanaimo's head hung low. It searched the dusky ground for grass.

Susan was torn. She wanted to deal with Nanaimo, but she also could see that Katerina was shaking and close to tears. Wulfric solved the problem for her. He gathered Nanaimo's reins and nodded toward Katerina. Meles led Katerina's horse away for a good rubdown.

Susan nodded, took a deep breath, and moved over to stand beside Katerina. She wasn't sure how to help. Katerina stood, stiff, hands clenched at her sides. She was staring straight ahead into the trees. Susan could tell from her breathing that she was trying not to cry. Tears trickled down Katerina's cheeks.

Susan reached out and put her arm around Katerina's shoulders. She drew her close, and Katerina sank into her arms. They sat together on a log.

"What happened?" Susan asked.

Katerina drew a shuddering breath. "It was the horses," she said and gulped. "I saw you looking at the harness, and I noticed the jingle sound of the one with the little silver medallions on it." She drew in a breath and held it for a moment. "Then I saw the top medallion. It was the cross of Saint George."

Susan shrugged. "Which saint is that?"

"The English one," Katerina answered like the weight of doom was on her.

Susan patted her hand. "Sir Robert can't be the only Englishman in Europe."

"But I looked further." Katerina shuddered. "The next medallion was the coat of arms of Robert's family. Then I knew. They were all in that inn. I had to get away."

Susan blew out her cheeks. "That was a close call." She patted Katerina's arm. "Do you still wish that you could marry Sir Robert?"

Katerina stared off into the distance for a moment. "That's impossible," she answered. Suddenly Katerina turned to Susan and grasped her arms. "I have to get to Lady Beatrice," she said. "If they catch me tomorrow, Frederick will walk into a trap. The whole world will suffer if Frederick isn't crowned emperor."

Bit dramatic, Susan thought. But she and Jason were still in this century, so there must be something else they had to do.

"There must be a way for you to jump me there. You jumped onto the boat to rescue me and then to that other camp." Katerina pounded her fist on her thigh. "Why won't you do it?"

Susan sighed. She could see Watt and Henri picking their way through the other campers searching for them. "Look," she said, putting as much emphasis as she could into her words. "I can't just jump to a place I've never been." She waved her hand around her head. "I have to picture the place in my head before I can go there."

Katerina was thinking now. "But you came for me. You didn't know what the boat would look like."

Susan nodded. "But I knew what you looked like, and I knew things about you. Not just how you looked but the way you walked and how you smile—and how you look when you're fierce. I put that all together and made a picture of you." Susan quirked her lips at the memory. "I wasn't even sure that would work. I'd never done it before."

Katerina fished around down the front of her tunic. She pulled out a silver locket. Using her fingernails and with her tongue between her teeth, she picked at the catch.

Finally it sprang open.

With a smile, Katerina held it out to Susan. "Meet my grandmother Beatrice," she said proudly.

Susan peered at the little picture inside the locket. It was definitely a picture of a woman, but the light was fading, and she could barely see any detail at all.

She moved over to stand close to the fire that Wulfric had set. Katerina brought a couple of candles over to augment the light.

As soon as he dismounted, Henri hurried over to the girls. "Eric, Peter, what happened back there?" he demanded.

Katerina took him by the arm and drew him away from Susan. "I'll explain."

Susan continued to stare at the tiny picture. Could she do this? Jump to a place she'd never been, drawn to a woman she'd never met? And drag other people with her? What if she failed and they all ended up in some gray fog that never changed? What if they all died?

She tried picking out the individual features of the lady. Her hair seemed blond; it was curled in the picture. Her face was thin, and she had a very narrow nose. The artist had painted her with a severe look. She stared straight ahead so that as Susan looked at her, she stared sternly back at Susan. This woman, this Lady Beatrice, looked like a force to be reckoned with.

The smell of cooked food broke into her concentration. She looked up to see that Serrill and Jason had arrived.

Jason shrugged. "I was hungry," he said with a grin.

Serrill gave him a look. "We went around to the kitchen door and got food for everyone," he said.

Jason handed her a chicken leg. Rosemary was sprinkled on the skin. It was roasted and still a little warm. Susan breathed in the aroma. Then she took a bite. Wonderful. *It is so easy to take food for granted when Mum plonks it on the table every meal,* she realized. *I'll have to thank her when I get home.*

For a while, they all sat around their campfire, gnawing chicken bones and munching bread.

Finally, with all the chicken bones thrown into the fire and everyone gathered around in a tight group, Susan wiped her greasy fingers down the side of her jeans and turned to the others. She had thought long and hard while she ate.

"Tell me everything you know about Lady Beatrice," she said.

Henri looked up, puzzled. "Why?"

"I need to know her very well. I want to try something, and I need to know Lady Beatrice as well as..." She waved her hand vaguely. "As well as I know Peter here."

Susan saw that Katerina understood immediately why she wanted the information. Katerina stared into the firelight as she gathered thoughts of her grandmother.

Henri stood. "Silly," he said, "we'll be there in a couple of days, and then you'll probably know more about her than you really want to." He turned to walk off.

Katerina jumped to her feet. "Henri, this is important to me. We're in a hurry. It is vital, to me that Eric hears everything you know about grandmother now."

Henri turned, surprised. He stood for a moment, looking at Katerina with new respect. Then he quietly sat back down in the fire circle. "Wulfric, Meles, you have never even seen Lady Beatrice. You keep watch," he ordered. Henri turned back to Susan. "What do you want to know?"

Indeed what did she want to know? Susan held tight to the locket. "Tell me how she walks and sits and smiles. That will be good for a start."

Henri thought for a moment. "She walks as though she's balancing her jewelry box on her head. Always so stiff and straight. She always sits in a straight-backed chair, never a stool, and she would still be balancing her jewels on her head, even sitting, unless she's reading, or sewing." He shook his head. "She never smiles."

Great. "How does she speak?"

Henri thought some more. "Loudly enough to be heard by the entire room when she wants to be. Quietly if she's telling you something she doesn't want others to hear. When she is angry, each word is clipped and precise. She never shouts. She never waves her arms around, but you know if she is unhappy with your actions."

"She speaks two languages fluently and gets by in two others," Katerina cut in. "She is in control of vast estates and several palaces. She has been a widow for many, many years, and it has fallen to her to further Frederick's interests in the Holy Roman Empire. She isn't always stiff and imperious."

Henri shrugged. "You defend her, but I'm telling about the woman I see. Yes, she is very capable. She wields a lot of influence and is greatly respected for her power, but she is a hard woman. You do not cross Lady Beatrice." He nodded at Katerina. "You know that better than most."

Susan raised her eyebrow at Katerina, who looked down at her shoes. "I wanted to attend the university in Salerno. Frederick made a large donation to keep the most knowledgeable tutors there."

"Only men attend universities," muttered Watt.

Katerina kicked his shin. "She wouldn't let me. She said that I needed to learn to control a palace. Hohenstaufens were meant for power, not to hide themselves away. Especially in some place where people sat around all day talking about what some dead person thought."

"Goodness!" Susan exclaimed.

Katerina continued. "That's why she sent me to stay in that Welf castle. 'Get to know your enemy,' she told me. 'Learn to keep a diplomatic tongue in your head,' she said."

Susan reached over and gave Katerina's arm a squeeze.

Watt spoke up next. "I only saw her once. She came to Frederick's court in Sicily to urge him to work toward becoming emperor." Watt shifted on the log. "I saddled her horse for her. They were going riding." He rubbed the side of his head. "She swatted me one. She didn't like the color of the saddle blanket I had spread on her horse."

Susan took a deep breath. *Crystal, take me home. I don't want to meet this person.* That's what she thought. What Susan did was hold out the locket. "Is this how she really looks?" she asked.

Watt peered at the tiny picture with his head to one side. He pulled a candle closer to get a really good look. "She was younger when this was painted," he said, handing it back. "Her hair is gray now, not like the lock in there."

Susan peered at the locket again. She hadn't taken any notice of the lock of hair coiled into the lid opposite the picture.

Katerina leaned in to peer at the hair also. "It is gray now, but you can see that it is very fine and a little curly." She waved her hands around her head. "She mostly covers her hair now anyway."

Susan closed her eyes and tried to picture this imperious person. *Can I do it? Can I conjure up a good enough picture of her so that the crystal can take me to her?* That was the question.

"Let's go." Katerina stood and turned to pull Susan to her feet. But Susan shook her head.

"I'm not sure this will work," she said. "I will not take anyone else until I know I can take you to her."

She stood facing Katerina, who put her hands on her hips.

"You did before," she said.

"Huh." Jason rubbed his head. "She tried it out on me first."

Susan looked around the circle of faces. "I will try it," she said. "I don't know whether I can do this, but I will try it." She walked off into the trees.

Jason caught up with her. "Don't let them push you into something you don't want to do."

Susan smiled at him. "I said I had to learn more about using the crystal. No good waiting for the instruction paper to tell me what to do. I'm going to try."

"Well, good luck. Just come back, all right."

"Oh, Jason. I just realized if I blow this, you're stuck here."

Jason shrugged. "Worse things have happened to me. I almost died as a child. No one knows how I survived. I have a charmed life, you know."

Susan looked around the place where they were standing. Trees surrounded them. She wasn't sure what kind of tree they were, but they stood tall and straight. The trunks shone gray and speckled in the firelight flickering through the trees. "Make sure

they all understand how they have to be joined together if they want to make the trip with us." She
patted Jason's shoulder, and he turned and walked
back to the circle.

Susan watched them for a moment through the
trees. It looked cozy and comfortable around the
fire. She sighed. This was what she had to do. She
fixed all her concentration on the miniature picture
in her hands. She let her eyes rove over the coil of
hair, and she thought about all the details the others
had told her about Lady Beatrice.

Finally, she looked deep into the crystal nestled in her palm. It sparkled and glowed orange as
though reflecting the firelight. *It's encouraging me.*
Susan drew in a deep breath. "Crystal, take me to
this person, this Lady Beatrice. Take me to her." The
swirling whirling began. "Please," she added.

Susan went somewhere.

She landed on a stone floor. She lost her balance
and fell onto all fours. The noise of her fall startled
the woman sitting in a chair by the fire. The woman
leaped to her feet.

Susan had just a moment to recognize Lady
Beatrice.

"Guards. Guards. Intruder," Lady Beatrice yelled
at the top of her voice.

Susan stood and started to explain. "I've come
from Katerina—" she began, but the door slammed

open, revealing two armed soldiers. Their swords were drawn, and they stood in the doorway, looking around to assess the threat.

When Susan turned her attention back to Lady Beatrice, she had picked up a metal pot on a long pole, and she was already swinging it in Susan's direction.

"Woah." Susan ducked and, without thinking, kicked out at the danger coming toward her. The pot burst open and coals sprayed out onto the carpet.

"Seize him," Lady Beatrice yelled, pointing at Susan. "Don't just stand there like doorposts. Seize him."

The soldiers advanced. They spread out so they were coming at her from either side. Susan was trapped.

She turned to the lady. "Katerina is my friend," she said. She grasped her crystal tight in her hand. She pictured the spot where she wanted to go. "Take me," she told the crystal.

It tingled in her hand. She was back in the forest. Her heart thumped. She took a deep breath. She took another. She waited until she could no longer feel her heart bumping.

A huge smile crept across her face. *I did it. Another thing I've learned. Thank you, crystal. I have some things of my own to write on the paper when I get home.*

She peeped through the trees. Things had changed around the fire since she left.

CHAPTER 47
FOUND!

The group were all on their feet. Henri looked angry. Jason looked amused. Watt had his hand on his sword hilt. Everyone stared at Katerina, and Katerina stared at the man who had joined the group.

Susan crept closer.

Katerina had her hand on the man's arm. "But how did you find me?" she asked. "I'm disguised as a boy."

Susan peered closely at the strange man.

The fire flared up, and in the brighter light, Susan recognized him.

Sir Robert smiled and pulled at his beard. "You can't disguise yourself from me, Katerina," he said. He hugged her shoulders. "I'll admit I wasn't quite sure." He chuckled. "But when I saw a rider turn and gallop away from the inn, I wondered why."

Katerina looked up at him. "But I didn't see you. I recognized the harness on your horse."

Robert nodded. "Yes, well, I was staring out of the upstairs window. Gustaff had called for a drink, and he and Klaus were swilling away, and I was missing you, and then I saw this person galloping away from the inn, and I watched. You can't disguise how you ride a horse, Katerina, even if you are wearing boy's clothing."

Katerina laughed and hugged Robert. Then quickly stood back to look at him again.

Robert put up his finger and wagged it at her. "And I'm sure you will recall this isn't the first time I've seen you dressed as a boy." They both laughed.

Henri had relaxed. Watt no longer held the hilt of his sword. Jason rolled his eyes at the moony looks on Katerina's and Robert's faces.

Susan drew a deep breath and took a step toward the group.

Wulfric tumbled into the firelight. With his hands tied behind and a gag in his mouth, he fell forward and hit his head on the stones surrounding the fire pit. Meles rushed to pull him back to safety, but every other eye in the group turned to Sir Gustaff and Sir Klaus, who stood at the shadow's edge. Both had their swords drawn.

"Well, well, what a pretty reunion," Sir Gustaff sneered. Sir Klaus nodded and chuckled.

Susan drew back into the trees.

Sir Gustaff bowed mockingly to Katerina. "Ah, lady," he smirked. "How glad I am to see you alive." He threatened the group with his sword. "We are on the way to bring tiding of your death to your grand-mother." He turned to Klaus. "Well, maybe we still will." Klaus grinned at him.

Everything happened so quickly in the next little while that Susan had to think about it later to get it all straight in her head.

Gustaff moved toward Katerina waving his sword threateningly. Sir Robert drew his sword and stepped in front of her. Katerina drew her knife.

Watt and Henri also sprang to stand in front of Katerina.

Jason moved up along the side to stand with the group.

Meles removed Wulfric's gag and untied his hands. Serrill moved over to join them. They began to creep backward into the trees, where Susan hid. *Trying to sneak around behind Gustaff and Klaus.*

Susan grabbed Serrill's hand. She put her fingers to her lips. They all squatted down together watch-ing the scene unfold around the fire.

"Sir Robert." Klaus came close to him. "You are a representative of His Majesty King John. Stop this nonsense. You are with us."

"Stay back." Robert grasped his sword two-handed and held it firm.

"Oh, leave him." Gustaff shrugged. "He can have an accident. Send a sad letter to the king. He'll send us someone better." Gustaff worked his shoulders. "Glad we didn't bring our soldiers. This is going to be fun." He advanced another step. He thumped his free hand on his chest. "I'm the biggest, the baddest, and we will rule this land."

"Yeah, yeah," Henri mocked.

Everyone braced themselves for a deadly fight.

Then Susan saw the way out.

She turned to Serrill, Wulfric, and Meles. "Hide among the other campers," she told them. "Don't fight. Bring the horses and everything along later."

The three looked surprised, but they nodded. Each touched her shoulder as they slipped off into the night. "It was a pleasure to know you, Eric—or whatever your name is," Serrill whispered as he passed.

Susan turned her attention back to the group around the fire. Yes, the positioning looked perfect. Their group all clustered around Katerina. Robert was a little in front, and Klaus was standing to the side. Gustaff was still a few metres away. The fight hadn't started yet.

It was easier for Susan to form a picture of Lady Beatrice and the room she had arrived in now that she had been there. It felt almost as though the lady's face was etched on the back of her eyeballs.

With the picture set in her mind and the crystal grasped firmly in her hand, she leaped to her feet. Let out a yell. "I'm here." And ran at the back of the crowd. Instinctively the group pulled together. Susan pushed Katerina in the back so that she fell forward against Henri and Watt. Watt jostled Jason, who gripped his arm for balance.

"Crystal, take us to Lady Beatrice," Susan yelled.

As the swirling of colors and sound began Susan heard two things.

Katerina sighed. "Beloved."

Sir Klaus cried, "Sir Robert, are you all right?"

Then the world was a swirl of colors and sounds. *I hope the guards have gone back to their posts,* she thought as she firmly kept their destination in mind. *We seem to be taking longer than usual. This is the most people I've moved.*

They arrived.

In front of a very startled Lady Beatrice.

CHAPTER 48

INTRODUCTIONS

That lady sprang to her feet again. The cup she held in her hand came sailing across the room and smashed into the wall beside Jason's head.

Susan drew back to the wall and tried to take in the scene. It was pretty chaotic.

Sir Robert hugged Katerina tight. "What happened?" He looked around. "Where are we?" He took a deep breath. "Don't worry, Katerina. I'll protect you."

"Guards, guards." Lady Beatrice was yelling again.

Henri made a deep bow toward the lady, and as soon as Watt noticed, he copied him. They both remained in deep bows.

Sir Klaus was down on all fours on the floor vomiting as though his heart was coming out.

Sir Klaus! What's he doing here?

The guards burst through the door. The same two as before.

They stood, stunned, in the doorway. So many people. Nobody had come past them.

"Wait. Wait." Katerina pulled away from Robert and stood tall. "Stop all this fuss," she ordered. "I am Lady Katerina, here for the Margrave of Bavaria. All will be explained." She turned to her grandmother. "We mean you no harm, and I have important and urgent news."

Everyone stood frozen for a moment.

Lady Beatrice stalked up to Katerina and peered at her face. She wrinkled her nose. "Your hair, child. What have you done to your hair?"

Katerina gave the hair just above her ear a nervous tug. "Um, I've been disguised as a boy, Grandmamma," she explained and bobbed a little curtsey.

Lady Beatrice turned her attention to Sir Robert. She peered down her nose at him, which was quite a feat as he was taller. "And who is this person? Gentleman? He is hanging on to you in a most impertinent manner."

Katerina turned and smiled at Robert, who clicked his heels and made a short bow to the lady. "He is Sir Robert, my betrothed," she said. She looked a question at him, and he nodded with a smile. "Well, not officially yet." She shrugged. "I had to leave the court in quite a hurry."

"Humph, we'll see," Lady Beatrice responded.

She moved along the line to the next person. Henri stood from his bow and inclined his head to her. "Aren't you a long way from the river?" she asked. "I hope that boat of yours hasn't sunk. I'm expecting a wine delivery."

Henri smiled. "All is well, madam. I just thought it would be best to escort Lady Katerina to you in the quickest way possible." Henri looked around for Susan. "Of course I didn't expect it to be quite this quick," he added.

Henri's glance attracted Lady Beatrice's attention to her. Susan stood a little straighter and tried to smooth down the front of her tunic. "You, boy, startled me. In and out of here in a flash." She flung her hand up. "Poof. Quite upset the guards." She wagged her finger at Susan. "I will require an explanation of your behavior, young man."

Katerina hurried over to stand beside Susan. She laughed. "Grandmamma, meet Susan. She has rescued me and helped me, and I wouldn't have made this journey successfully without the help of her and her faithful companion, Jason."

Susan bobbed a curtsey as she had seen Katerina do.

"Her? Her!" Lady Beatrice looked Susan up and down. "This is a her, in her odd blue leggings and scruffy tunic?" She shook her head. "Disgraceful, two girls traipsing across the country, no chaperones, disguised as boys." She turned to Katerina. "This behavior has got to stop."

At that moment, Sir Klaus threw up again. He'd managed to make quite a mess.

Sir Robert stepped forward. "Um, madam, this is Sir Klaus." He pointed at that sorry knight where he hunched on the floor. "The trip here appears to have left his stomach in turmoil."

Lady Beatrice looked at him for a moment. "Yes, it's all turmoil here." She turned to the guards standing in the doorway. "We will move to the meeting hall. Have refreshments brought there," she ordered. She waved her hands at the room. "Get someone to clean up this mess." She pointed to Sir Klaus. "And get him put somewhere comfortable until he is fit for company."

Lady Beatrice stood a moment and looked around the group. "Come," she said and stalked out of the room.

The others hurried to follow.

Susan heard Sir Klaus heaving again as she left the room. *Crystal travel has never affected me like that. Thank goodness.*

Jason caught up with her as they hurried along. "We're still here. We got Katerina to her grandmother, and we're still here."

Susan nodded. "Keep close. There must be something else. Another danger." Susan looked around. "Katerina should be safe now."

CHAPTER 49

REFRESHMENT SURPRISES

Lady Beatrice led them along a passageway, down a long flight of stone steps, and into a vast hall.

Susan couldn't swivel her head fast enough to take it all in. The roof stretched way above her head. Oil lamps shone from scones attached to the walls. More oil lamps burned on a long table, which stretched down the center of the room. Benches and stools lined the sides of the table. *This looks like a dining hall*, Susan decided. Her feet scuffed in rushes on the floor.

As they moved through the hall, Susan noticed another table, which stood at right angles to the first. This one was raised higher. A large carved and cushioned chair was placed in the center spot.

"Looks like a throne from a movie," Jason whispered in her ear.

"That's where Lady Beatrice sits for formal meals," Henri told them. "I saw you looking." He came up to join the pair. "Closest to the fireplace is the most comfortable place in winter."

Lady Beatrice clapped her hands. Two servants sprang to open a set of double doors situated on one side of the fireplace. She swept through, the others followed, and the servants closed the doors again.

The table in this room was smaller. Susan estimated that it would seat ten people comfortably. Cushioned chairs and couches ranged at either end of the room. They were set around small tables. They formed areas where a few people could sit for a relaxed chat.

The best part of the room, though, was the windows. Two large windows occupied one wall of the room. Curious, Susan sidled over to have a look. Jason followed her. The windows were comprised of small panes of glass held together by metal strips. *Like a church window.* Susan ran her finger down one of the strips. The glass wasn't perfect. There were knobby bits in it so that their view was a little distorted in places.

What they could see was magnificent. "Look at the lake." Jason pointed. Susan nodded. The sun had risen over the distant hills. A rosy glow lit the lake nestled in the valley. *We've been up all night. No wonder I feel so tired.*

"Sit."

The imperious order startled Susan into alertness. She and Jason turned to see the rest of the group sitting in chairs or on the floor clustered around Lady Beatrice. That lady sat ramrod straight in a high-backed chair. Her feet were perched on a pillow, and her arms lay along the arms of the chair. *She acts like a queen,* Susan noticed. *Or maybe the grandmother of an emperor.*

Susan and Jason hurried over to the group and found places on the floor next to Watt. Katerina and Robert sat on a couch. They were holding hands. Henri occupied another chair, his legs crossed. He looked at ease.

Lady Beatrice nodded once in satisfaction. "Now. Explanations." She pointed at Susan. "You first."

Susan blinked in surprise. "Um," she said. "I only meant to bring Katerina, Henri, Watt, and Jason."

"I grabbed Robert. I wanted him to come, too," Katerina piped up, smiling at Robert, who brought her hand to his lips and kissed it.

Jason groaned.

Robert took up the story. "I didn't know what was happening when things went twirly. I staggered a little, and Sir Klaus took my arm to steady me, so he came along, too." Robert shrugged, "That's all I know. I'm not even sure where here is—except that Katerina is here."

Susan jabbed Jason in the ribs before he could groan again.

Lady Beatrice looked around the group. "I want an explanation for this disturbance," she said. "Katerina, what is the meaning of this? First, you can't leave the Welf court, and then you're escaping and madcapping all through the empire with these people. What folly have you jumped into?"

Katerina stood. "Grandmamma," she began. She flicked her fingers, not sure how to continue. "I overheard a dreadful plot to assassinate Frederick. He had no way of knowing and would have walked into a dreadful trap."

Lady Beatrice tutted. She waved her hand in dismissal. "There are always plots. Why didn't you send that boy there?" She pointed at Watt. "That one with no color sense. He could have brought the plot to Frederick's attention."

Katerina nodded and plopped herself down on the couch again. "But they suspected that I had heard them. They would have found a way for me to have an accident."

Sir Robert had sat with his mouth open throughout Katerina's tale. "Katerina, you should have come to me. I would have protected you. Surely you know that."

Katerina shook her head. "You are Sir Robert. Emissary of King John of England in the court of the Welfs. How could you help me without causing no end of trouble?"

Lady Beatrice hammered her fist on the arm of her chair. "King John. You represent that addlepated nincompoop?" She pointed at Katerina. "What were you thinking?"

"I was thinking that I needed to get away from the Welfs and warn Frederick," Katerina declared. "The children came through the town, and I saw that as my chance to slip away. Watt helped me."

"You mean these pilgrim children that we hear about?" Lady Beatrice wanted to know.

Katerina nodded. "I hid among them, with Watt. We traveled a little way with them. They helped us in many ways."

"Then what happened?"

"Susan and Jason happened." Katerina smiled at the two sitting comfortably on the floor.

Lady Beatrice wriggled in her chair. "Humph," she acknowledged. "Yes, well, it all seems to have worked out. You're here now." She rang the bell standing on the table next to her chair. "I called for refreshments. Where are they?" She looked to the door. It didn't open. She glared around at the group. "There's a lot more to this story yet, and I intend to hear it all, understand?"

A knock at the door saved them all from more glaring.

Soldiers pushed the door open, and a servant staggered in, carrying a huge tray. Susan smelled bacon. She saw a loaf of bread so fresh from the oven that steam rose from it in a wisp. The servant carried the tray forward and, keeping his head lowered respectfully, set it down on the table near the group. The food looked wonderful. Susan couldn't take her eyes off the bowl of boiled eggs sitting on the tray next to the bacon. The servant kept his head down as he sliced the steamy bread into thick slices. Eager hands grabbed each plate as soon as a slice from his knife fell on it.

A plate? Susan tapped at hers with her finger. *Not china.* She tapped again. *Metal.*

Jason forked a piece of bacon onto his bread, looked around, and forked another on top. "I am so hungry." He sighed.

Watt chuckled. "You're always hungry."

Watt was the last to receive a plate from the servant. As Watt reached for it, the servant jostled his hand. Watt looked up and gasped. He leaped to his feet and immediately fell to one knee. He bowed his head. "Sire," he said.

At that one word and Watt's reaction, everyone looked up startled. Henri leaped to his feet, and then he also dropped to one knee. "Sire," he echoed.

Susan and Jason looked at each other. Susan lifted her eyebrow. Jason shrugged with a smile, and the two of them shimmied from their sitting positions into a shaky, one-kneed kneel. They kept their heads down.

"What are you doing here?" Lady Beatrice carefully placed her plate on the table and scowled across the bowed heads at the servant—who was obviously not a servant.

At her grandmother's question, Katerina drew her eyes away from Robert for a moment. She peered at the servant closely. She squealed, jumped to her feet, and ran to give him a hug. "Frederick, you're safe." She hugged him harder.

Susan and Jason exchanged looks. Frederick? Susan screwed up her nose and sank back onto the floor, too tired to maintain a kneeling position. Jason did the same.

Lady Beatrice rapped on the arm of her chair. "Enough of this nonsense. What are you doing here?"

Frederick moved Katerina to the side and addressed his grandmother. "Ah, Grandmamma, how you do get to the nub of the matter." He swept her a mocking bow.

"Humph."

"Sit, sit." Frederick made motions with his hands. Katerina moved back to her place on the couch.

Henri dusted off his seat and gestured Frederick into it. Watt hurried to pull up a chair for Henri.

There was a moment's pause as everyone settled back into their places. Everyone looked at everyone else. It was not every morning that the emperor brought you your breakfast.

Frederick wriggled into his seat and casually crossed his legs. "Now, Katerina," he began, "I notice that you are sitting next to a person whom I do not know."

Katerina smiled at Robert and turned to introduce him.

"Oh, he's the English emissary from that dunce John," Lady Beatrice interjected. "Now, what are you doing here, Frederick?" She waved her finger. "I won't ask you again."

Frederick nodded. Susan noticed that he was hiding a smile. "Well, I thought I would just slip in quietly to see how the good burghers of Lake Konstanz were reacting to the news of my up-coming investiture as emperor." He bowed to Lady Beatrice. "I had heard that you were doing so well in convincing them it would be wise to support me."

"Humph."

Frederick turned to Katerina. "I also heard that you were traveling to visit Grandmamma under quite unusual circumstances and that you had important information that you could only entrust to me."

Katerina frowned. "How did y—"

"Griswald sent a messenger to inform me," Frederick explained. "He said that Henri was bringing you here along the river. I didn't see any boat tied up when I arrived late last night." Frederick raised his eyebrows at Henri.

Henri bobbed his head in acknowledgment. "Our plans required adjusting along the way, sire," he said.

Katerina laughed. "Yes, lots of adjusting. I wouldn't be here or anywhere but dead if it wasn't for Jason and Susan, who have been my staunch companions along the way."

All eyes turned to where Jason and Susan sat on the floor. Susan tried to stifle the yawn, which was just too big to hide.

"They're children," Frederick exclaimed.

Lady Beatrice rang the little bell beside her table. "Powerful children, it seems," she said.

A servant entered the room.

"Find comfortable beds for these children right now. Make sure they have everything they need." Lady Beatrice looked to where Susan and Jason were drooping on the floor. "Although it looks as though sleep is what they need the most."

Frederick stood. "Find rooms for everyone," he said. "Katerina, you and I must talk. Now." He sauntered from the room, and Katerina hurried to catch up.

The servant looked around. Lady Beatrice backed up the order. "You heard the man, Gaston. Get these people to bed."

Gaston nodded and led the way from the room. They all followed like a gaggle of ducklings, leaving Lady Beatrice sitting alone and thoughtful in her very straight-backed chair.

CHAPTER 50
WORRY

"Susan, wake up."

Susan opened one eye.

Katerina shook her shoulder again. "Get up. I've got a surprise for you."

Susan rolled over and gave a wonderful stretch. She lay in a comfortable bed, fluffy pillows under her head. A wonderful perfume filled the air.

Susan breathed in deeply. *Flowers. I smell flowers.*

Katerina pushed aside the drapes that covered the large window. Golden sunlight swept into the room. Susan pulled the covers up to her chin.

Katerina threw a pillow at her head. "Come on. Get up," she insisted. "You've slept a day and a night."

"Yeah, yeah." Susan rolled over and put her feet to the floor. In front of the fireplace stood a large barrel...Well, not exactly a barrel. It was more oval shaped than round and looked as though it had been cut in half. Spilled water lay on the floor. Steam wafted from it. Susan took another deep breath. The air smelled wonderful.

"Lavender." Katerina ushered her over to the barrel. "You always kept talking about wanting a bath, so I got one ready for you."

"Wonderful." Susan dropped her tunic and struggled out of her jeans. "The water's hot." She sank into the little tub with a sigh.

Katerina handed her a piece of soap and left a towel draped over the back of a chair. "Don't be too long. I let you sleep as long as I could. We have a lot to do this day."

"Really?" Susan sighed. "More stuff?" Then she had a thought. "Where's Jason?"

Katerina chuckled. "Oh, he's busy right now. He'll see you later." She firmly shut the door behind her as she left.

Susan sighed again. *Hurry, hurry, hurry. That's all I've been doing for days.* The soap slipped from her fingers, and she had to grope for it in the tub.

As she stood drying herself, the door burst open, and there stood Katerina, this time followed by a bevy of young maids. They were loaded down with bundles and boxes, which they dumped onto the bed.

Katerina made shooing movements with her hands, and all the girls and ladies hurried out of the room again. Susan heard little giggles as Katerina shut the door behind them.

"I thought you would still be soaking in the tub." Katerina rubbed her hands together. "Come on now. I've brought you some decent clothes to wear." She held up a long dress and swung it around. "It's lucky you and I are about the same size." Katerina thrust the dress toward Susan. "Try this," she said.

Susan slipped the dress over her head. It fell loose and long on her. The fabric between her fingers felt slightly scratchy. It was tightly woven. The dress was a pretty pink.

"We use the skins of beetroot to make that color," Katerina informed her.

Susan buried her face in the skirt and took a deep breath.

"We put lavender into our storage chests," Katerina explained.

And that's how the day progressed. Everything was new to Susan, and Katerina took great pleasure in explaining every detail of her life in a palace.

Jason joined them at breakfast, but they had little chance to chat together until later in the afternoon when they were able to wander in the garden within the walls.

"We're still here." Jason started right in.

Susan frowned. "I'm worried about it," she acknowledged. "Something else must be going to happen." She spread her hands. "But what?"

Jason shrugged. "It seems so peaceful here."

"Frederick isn't what I thought an emperor would be like. Maybe it's something to do with that."

Jason grinned. "He certainly jokes around more than I thought an emperor would." They found a seat in an arbor of climbing roses. "Still, he's only nineteen years old."

"Really? I knew he was young, but that's very young to have so much responsibility on your shoulders."

"Watt told me," Jason said. "Frederick was king of Sicily when he was three, so I guess he's used to it."

Susan laughed.

"What's so funny?"

She shook her head. "I'm just remembering a three-year-old pharaoh, who got dragged around and painted up and could really throw a tantrum with the best of them."

Jason nodded. "Huh."

"Watt told me that Frederick intends to campaign with all the important people in the town while he's here. Meeting after meeting. Maybe that's going to cause the trouble."

Susan looked around as though there were an enemy over her shoulder. "I just feel that it's all building up to something. I hope I'm going to be able to fix it."

Jason jostled her shoulder. "You talk about all these other people having responsibility when they're young. Look at you."

"There you are." Katerina stood in front of them, hands on hips. "I was wondering where you had got to."

The two jumped to their feet.

"Just resting," they said together. Looked at each other and laughed.

Joining hands with Katerina, they all walked off along the garden path.

━━◁ ▷━━

Within the palace, the days seemed to meld into one another. They were always busy. There was a lot to do and see and learn, but at all times Susan felt that she should be looking over her shoulder. More trouble was coming, and she had no idea how to stop it or keep everyone safe.

Jason caught her mood and tried to stay as close to her as possible.

The thought of leaving Jason behind and having to explain to her family where he was, just added to her worry.

And so the days wore on.

Katerina and Robert spent every spare moment together, sitting in a nook, walking the ancestor galleries of the palace, tossing a ball to each other in the garden. Susan watched their love grow. *They will be happy together.* Susan was sure.

Sir Klaus skulked about. He didn't look happy, but he explored the palace and entered into games in the evening. Susan knew he was free to leave at any time, but he didn't.

Frederick kept busy. Every morning, important people from the towns and countryside around Lake Konstanz would be ushered quietly into the palace. They met with the soon-to-be-crowned emperor behind closed doors. Mostly they left with handshakes, deep bows, and smiles. In the afternoon, Frederick would sit with Lady Beatrice and other advisors. But as evening drew in, he would join the others for the evening meal and then for the games and discussions that filled the hours before bedtime.

It was at these times that Susan felt the hairs on her neck bristle. Something was not right. She searched the faces of the crowd around her, but nothing looked out of place or wrong. As the days wore on, Susan's disquiet grew. She could feel that in this crowd of smiling, laughing people there was at least one person who was not happy to see Frederick anointed as emperor. She kept close to Jason.

CHAPTER 51
PREPARATION

Susan dunked her head for the third time, but suds still clung to her hair. The door opened again, and a maid entered. She carried two full buckets of water. She bobbed a curtsey to Susan. "More hot water for you, miss," she said and moved to the tub to empty the buckets.

"Wait, wait, I've got a better idea." Susan put her hand up. She explained what she wanted.

"Oh no, miss." The maid shook her head. "We don't do that."

Susan waved her hand about, pulling on her experience as an Egyptian princess. "It is done where I come from," she insisted. "Now, pull the chair over and stand on it," she ordered. Susan stood up in the tub. "Now, slowly pour the water over my head."

"But, but, this is so disrespectful," the maid protested. "What if Lady Beatrice sees what I'm doing?"

"Just do it," Susan insisted. "It's cold standing here wet. Slowly now. I need to get the soap out of my hair."

"Yes, miss." The servant gently poured the water over Susan's head. With the first bucket Susan managed to rinse all the suds from her hair. The water from the second sluiced over her shoulders and down her back. Wonderful. *Huh, I'm having the world's first shower.*

The door swung open, and Katerina marched in, followed by a gaggle of maids, all with bundles in their arms.

The maid on the chair squeaked and sloshed the rest of the bucket over Susan. Water went everywhere.

Katerina stopped up short. "Making a mess, I see." She tapped her foot. "Out now. We're in a hurry."

The maid climbed down off the chair. "She made me, Lady Katerina. She made me."

Katerina patted the girl's arm. "It's all right, Maddie. Lady Susan has some funny ideas about how things should be done." Katerina pushed her gently toward the door. "Go down to the kitchen and dry off now."

In the meantime, Susan had stepped from the tub and dried herself quickly. By the time the door shut behind Maddie, Susan was dry but wrapped in a wet cloth.

"Sorry about the mess," she said.

Katerina flapped her hands in dismissal. "Sit over there," she ordered. "We have a lot to do to get you ready."

Susan sat. A covered dish stood on the bench in front of her. She smelled bacon. She lifted the cover. Toasted bread, eggs, bacon.

Susan cracked the shell on one of the boiled eggs. As she ate, she watched the activity around her.

Someone mopped the floor. Another lady had spread interesting-looking clothing all over the bed. Susan turned back to the plate for a piece of bacon.

"Jessica, see what you can do with her hair before it dries," Katerina ordered. Another lady, Jessica, bobbed a curtsey and began to carefully comb through Susan's hair.

"It's too short," she murmured.

"I like it that way," Susan retorted.

Over the next little while, Susan's hair was put into order and lotion rubbed into her hands and arms.

Susan watched Katerina. It was interesting to notice the change in her. She was full of confidence. She knew what to say and do. She ordered the maids and servants around with a quiet authority. *This is her place*, Susan realized. *This is what she has been trained for. She looks so relaxed now.*

Katerina came over to where Susan sat. "I have to leave to get ready myself," she said. "These ladies will help you to dress." She turned toward the door.

"What are we getting ready for?"

Katerina turned. "Oh, there's going to be a celebration. Frederick decided to make it public that he's in Lake Konstanz, so there will be a big reception in the main hall, and we will be there."

Susan nodded, taking in the information. "Will your father, the Margrave of Bavaria, be there?"

Katerina looked startled for a moment, and then she burst out laughing. "Oh, Susan, there is no Margrave of Bavaria. We use that name as a recognition signal between Hohenstaufen supporters."

Susan looked down. "Oh," was all she said. Now she felt silly.

Katerina put her arms around her. "Don't feel bad, please. I wouldn't be here if it wasn't for your help." She gave Susan a squeeze. "You are honored here. You'll see."

With a quick glance back and a smile, Katerina hurried from the room.

Jessica curtsied in front of her. "Stand, please, lady. We need to have you ready in time."

Susan stood. *Well, this is going to be a different experience than the last big ceremony I attended.* Her mind drifted back to a certain hot day, on the plains of Egypt, where she had been a part of the dedication ceremony for Akheperenre's temple.

⊶ ⊷

The women fussed and pulled and tucked. They dropped a light, silky dress over her shoulders. Susan stroked the smoothness of the long sleeves against her skin. After wearing the slightly scratchy every-day clothes, this dress felt light and airy. The dark blue shimmered in the light from the window. Susan twirled around. The ladies laughed.

They dropped a heavier dress over the top of the first one. Susan ran her hands down the length of her body. This was stiffer material. Droopy bits hung from her elbows so that the dark blue of her under-dress poked through slits. She picked up one of the droopy bits to examine the material.

"That's all the way from Damascus, that is." One of the ladies stroked the fabric. "They call it dam-ask," she added, holding the fabric up to Susan's face. "See how they weave a pattern in with shiny and not shiny." Susan peered closely at the material and saw a pattern of interwoven flowers and leaves.

I've seen this at home. We have some placemats that mum uses on the dining room table when guests come.

She laughed and twirled again. *Look at me, Judy. I'm looking good in a tablecloth.*

But what she was wearing was much, much more than a tablecloth. The overdress was woven in a turquoise color, which balanced against the darker blue of the underskirt, to make her feel very regal.

Next the ladies fastened a golden chain around her waist. They didn't tighten it, but they fussed a little to get it to sit exactly right.

Susan wished for a mirror. *I would love to see what I look like. The clothes are so different from everything I ever wore in Egypt or at home, but I get the same feeling from them. I want to hold my head up and walk proudly.*

A knock on the door drew everyone's attention. The door swept open, and there stood Katerina. She looked magnificent. Her underdress was the dark green of a fir tree and her overdress was the color of leaves when the sun shines through them. Perched on her head was a golden circlet. Katerina smiled. The ladies swept into deep curtsies at her arrival.

She looks like a queen. Susan almost curtsied, too.

"Good, you're ready," Katerina said, gliding into the room. "I've brought you this." Katerina held out another golden circlet for Susan. "Grandmamma opened her jewelry chest for the occasion." Katerina grinned.

"Oh." Susan was tempted. "I don't think I should." *I must be going to leave soon, and I don't want to disappear with some royal heirloom that was only lent to me on my head.*

Katerina looked disappointed, but she placed the circlet on the bench and turned to take Susan's arm. "Let's join the celebration," she said.

Susan took a step and tripped. Oops. Long skirt.

Katerina smiled and shook her head. "Hold it in one hand like this." She demonstrated.

Susan grasped a part of the skirt, held it up, and the two of them sailed out of the room, laughing.

CHAPTER 52
THE CEREMONY

Even before they reached the main hall, Susan heard the sound of conversations and guessed that a large crowd had gathered.

As she and Katerina approached, guards clicked their heels and hurried to pull open the large doors. Susan stopped short in the doorway. The hall was packed with people. All were standing. The long tables and benches were stacked against the walls. Susan saw little conversational groups chatting together. Others just stood, obviously waiting for something to happen.

Somebody, somewhere, struck a gong. All eyes turned to the door where they stood. Susan and Katerina both took a deep breath at the same time, noticed, and grinned at each other.

"Here we go." Katerina stepped out into the crowd. Susan stepped with her.

And the crowd parted, leaving an open way through for them to walk. People murmured and smiled as they slowly paced toward the dais set up in front of the fireplace. Men bowed, and women curtsied. All smiled. Katerina drifted along, acknowledging everyone as she passed. Many told her how happy they were to meet her. They hoped her stay would be a long one.

"Psst." Susan turned her head and stopped short. There stood Serrill, Wulfric, and Meles. They all wore big grins. Wulfric had his hands behind his back. She rushed over to them. "I'm so glad to see you safe," she said.

They nodded. Serrill shuffled his feet. "What could Sir Gustaff do when you all disappeared and there was nobody left?"

"Temper, temper. He started smashing the tents." Wulfric took up the story. "We released their horses and set them on the road back to the inn, so he had to walk."

Meles butted in. "Then he found our horses and tried to climb onto Nan...Nan..." He waved his arm. "Your horse."

Susan gasped. "What happened?"

Serrill took up the story. "Nanaimo bit him, trod on his foot, and then galloped off a ways."

They all laughed. "We have him here," Serrill assured her. "He's snug in the stable."

Meles nodded. "Good horse."

The other two pushed Wulfric out in front of them. With a sheepish grin, he held out Susan's bag. "I knew that you always carried it. It was important to you," he said.

"What you want with an empty bag, though, I don't know." Serrill shrugged.

Susan caught her breath. *Empty?* She pushed her hand into the bag. Her fingers caught on the folding scissors. It felt as though everything was there. *Another mystery.*

"Thank you." She smiled at the three.

She slung the bag, right then, over her fancy dress. "It is so valuable to me," she said.

"Glad," Wulfric answered.

Katerina tugged at her arm. "We're delaying the ceremony," she said.

"We'll talk later," she assured the trio and moved on toward the dais.

As soon as they reached the top of the dais, Katerina hurried over to stand next to Sir Robert. They clasped hands and smiled at each other.

Susan paused and took note of the people there.

Sir Klaus stood beside Sir Robert. He had some color in his cheeks again. His arms were folded across his chest. He stared straight ahead. *He doesn't look happy to be here*, Susan noticed. The thought made her grin.

The Lady Beatrice, looking proud, was seated beside an empty chair. Jason stood just to the right of Lady Beatrice. He wore a broad grin as she moved toward him. "Don't you look all fancy," he mocked gently.

"Who is this knight standing next to me?" she mocked back. She looked around. "Where's Jason?"

They banged elbows. Jason leaned forward to whisper in her ear. "I've got stockings on, and they're kept up with strings tied around my waist," he said.

Susan looked at him sideways. "Well, I hope they don't fall down," she said. "And," she added in a whisper, "I've got no underpants. I asked, and the ladies laughed at me."

Jason raised his eyebrows at her. "Well, I hope you don't fall down," he said.

They both put their heads down to try to hide their laughter.

Trumpets sounded. A big fanfare. Loud.

All conversation stopped. All heads turned toward the door. It didn't open.

Susan heard a slight scuffle to her left.

"Ahem." Another scuffle. "Ahem." Louder this time.

Gradually, people's heads turned back toward the dais. The empty chair was now occupied.

Frederick stood. "Thank you all for coming."

People gasped. Frederick spread his arms. "Yes, it's me. I'm here."

The room fell to its knees.

"Always did like a showy entrance," Lady Beatrice muttered.

Frederick waved his hands. "Get up, get up." He looked around the room as people climbed back to their feet. "We're all friends here," he said. But Susan noticed a slight question in his voice.

Frederick raised his voice above the scuffling. "I am meeting with the good burghers of this town. I want you all to know me, your new emperor. I will be anointed later this year, and I want you to rejoice with me."

Lady Beatrice tapped her fingernail on the arm of her chair.

Frederick turned to her and bowed low. "Of course, Grandmother. Of course." He turned back to his audience. "I will have time to meet with you all in the next few days. Right now, I have an important duty to perform." He nodded to Katerina. "It's my pleasure to see it done." He smiled and beckoned.

Katerina squeezed Robert's hand and moved to stand beside Frederick. Then she leaned back and winked at Susan behind Frederick's back.

"Uh-oh," Jason whispered to her. "Something's up."

Susan nodded slowly. "Keep close."

"This is my dear cousin Katerina," Frederick began. "She has traveled across our empire to bring me news of an assassination plot."

A murmur ran through the crowd.

Frederick nodded solemnly. "Yes." He let the word hang. "People who want to bring the Holy Roman Empire to the brink of war with Italy are plotting to have me killed."

More murmurs.

"Ahem." Lady Beatrice made "get on with it" gestures with her hands.

"Er, yes," Frederick continued. "She was helped along her way by two strangers to our land. She tells me"—he smiled down fondly at Katerina—"that she would have been captured and killed without the help of these two children."

He turned to where the two stood, a little shy, a little embarrassed. "Come forward, Jason of Adelaide," Frederick commanded.

Susan gave Jason a gentle shove forward. He walked to the emperor.

"Kneel," was the command. Jason did so. On one knee. And he bowed his head.

Frederick drew his sword and held it aloft. Jason hunched his shoulders.

Susan moved to hurry forward.

"Stay," Lady Beatrice whispered to her. She was smiling, Susan saw.

Frederick tapped Jason gently on each shoulder with his sword. "By my power, I dub thee a knight of my realm." Jason looked up in surprise.

Frederick smiled and reached down to pull him to his feet. "Rise, Sir Jason of Adelaide." Once Jason stood, Frederick clasped him in a big hug. Katerina did, too.

Susan's smile stretched right across her face. What an honor. Good for Jason.

He walked back to stand beside Susan. His knees seemed a little shaky, but his smile was as wide as hers. Cheering started in the audience. Susan couldn't be sure, but it seemed to start with Serrill. The rest of the crowd joined in.

Frederick waved his hands for silence, and gradually the crowd settled down. *They're wondering what will come next*, Susan supposed.

Frederick turned to her and beckoned.

Susan gasped. She remembered to hold up her skirts and moved forward. *At least there's no cushions to trip over here*, she thought to herself.

She bobbed a nervous curtsey as she stood in front of Frederick.

He turned her to face the audience. "This child," he declared, "has rendered great service to our crown. She has several times rescued my cousin Katerina from harm and even death. She is beloved of my family and of me."

He turned her to face him again. "Kneel," he said. And then he grinned when he saw the look of dismay on Susan's face. He nodded and smiled.

Susan lifted her skirts and sank onto one knee in front of the emperor.

Out came his sword again. Light touches on her shoulders. "I dub you a knight of my realm," Frederick intoned. "It is a great pleasure for me to bestow on you all the lands I hold in the district of Swabia. Their revenues are yours. The people of Swabia will bow in deference to you. Rise, Lady Knight of Nanaimo."

Susan tried to stand, but somehow her foot got all tangled in her skirts. She began to topple. Frederick sheathed his sword and reached forward to steady her. Susan looked up at him. "You said Nanaimo."

Frederick laughed. "I practiced." He reached out his other hand and braced himself to haul Susan to her feet.

With Frederick's hands occupied and slightly off-balance with Susan's weight, Sir Klaus chose that moment to draw a knife and rush forward toward the emperor.

"Otto forever," he cried with his knife held up ready to stab.

Jason was quicker, though. He leaped across the platform and tackled Klaus around the knees. Over they both tumbled in a tangle of arms and legs. One scream, long and shrill, issued from the pair.

Susan stood transfixed. "Jason," she called softly.

The room erupted into noise and action after that one moment of silence. Ladies screamed. Men shouted. Many crowded the exits. Robert and Frederick rushed to the two sprawled on the floor. Sir Robert lifted Jason's shoulders and rolled him gently to the side. Susan scanned him quickly. No blood. She sighed with relief.

However, a pool of blood was seeping out from under Sir Klaus. Frederick rolled him onto his back. All could see he had fallen on his own knife.

"Why?" Frederick asked.

Sir Klaus gulped and drew a ragged breath. "Otto promised to make me pope," he whispered.

"And you believed him?"

Sir Klaus gasped. He screwed his face with pain. "I hoped." He sighed a sigh that rattled in his throat.

Frederick looked up at the crowd. "He's dead," he announced.

Susan felt a tingle. Her crystal. She'd left it in her room.

She rushed to Jason's side. "Quickly. Are you all right?"

He nodded, rubbing his shoulder. "Rugby tackle. Learned it at school," he muttered.

Frederick lifted Jason to his feet and enveloped him in a huge hug. "Once again you have done service to my crown."

Susan quietly held her hand out and commanded her crystal to come to her.

"What boon can I grant you?" Frederick asked.

Jason glanced at Susan and saw her hold up the crystal for him to see.

He nodded and sidled toward her. He rubbed his head again. "Um, nothing for me," he said. "What I would like you to do is help the children pilgrims. They are walking to the shore in Italy. They expect the sea to open for them so they can walk to Jerusalem. Help them, please."

Frederick stroked his beard for a moment. Then he nodded. "I will speak to the good people of Genoa. They need workers. They will offer a home to all who wish to stay. I can do no more," he vowed.

Susan grabbed for Jason's arm. "Thank you all," she called. "We must go now." The swirling had started. The colors were merging together. All the yelling and shouting in the hall was melding into one sound. Everything was blurry.

Katerina moved forward. "I can't touch you," she said. "I am where I am supposed to be. Thank you for all your help. I will never forget you."

Susan smiled. "Goodbye. I've learned a lot from you."

Then she surrendered to the crystal's pull, and she and Jason landed flat on the carpet in her bedroom.

CHAPTER 53

HOME

Susan sat up. "You saved Emperor Frederick's life."
Jason rubbed his shoulder. "I hope that was a good thing." He looked around her room. "Have you got any liniment? I haven't done a rugby tackle for a very long time."

Susan stood and stretched. "Don't you think we should change first?"

Jason got to his feet, and they stood side by side, looking at each other in Susan's full-length mirror.

"Well, don't we look the pair?"

Susan nodded. "We are the pair. Do you realize that we are now knights of the Holy Roman Empire?" She shook his hand with a smile. "Congratulations, Sir Jason of Adelaide."

"First dibs on the shower." Jason moved to the door.

Susan nodded. "OK, I'll use Mum and Dad's, but check that the family are still outside."

Jason opened the door slowly and slipped out into the family room. Susan turned to her cupboard to see what she had to wear. *I've lost my jeans and a pair of runners. How am I going to explain that?*

By the time Jason entered the family room, Susan was sitting in front of the jigsaw puzzle. So much had happened to them, and yet the table was exactly as they had left it. "I found another border piece," she said.

She looked up when Jason didn't answer.

He wore pajamas. His face looked ashen. He was holding himself up in the doorframe.

Susan leaped to her feet, knocking over the jigsaw table. She rushed to his side.

"I'm back where I was," Jason whispered.

Susan didn't know what to say. She put her arms around his shoulders and helped him to the couch. "Jason, I'm so sorry for dragging you off to Europe when you should have been here, quietly recovering."

Jason gripped her hand. "Never say that," he said. "It was an adventure. I felt wonderful. I thought I would never feel that way again, and you've shown me that it is possible." He patted his chest. "I'm a knight of the Holy Roman Empire. You're a lady knight. What an adventure." He shook his head. "I'm going to miss Watt and Katerina and all the others." Jason lay back on the cushions. "But now that we're back, would you please fetch my medication? I'm a bit late for my next dose." He started to laugh, but it turned into a cough. Susan hurried to the bathroom for water.

The phone rang.

Susan answered it after handing Jason his water and his pills. Reaching for the phone seemed so normal.

"Hello, Susan speaking."

"G'day. I need to speak to Ms. Laura Sinclair. Is she there?"

"Yes, she's here, but she's outside in the yard. Can she call you back?"

"Better not. There's a time problem. Go get her. I'll wait."

"Who will I say is calling?"

"Tell her it's Ray Spalding from the Grey Institute. She applied to have her son participate in our experimental cancer program. A position has opened up."

"Right, right, wait." Susan dropped the phone and ran.

She puffed up to the family. They were sipping lemonade in the shade of the maple tree. "Aunt Laura, come quick. There's someone on the phone from some institute about a cancer experiment."

Aunt Laura and Uncle John both jumped to their feet. Hope bloomed in their eyes. "The Grey Institute?"

Susan nodded. "Yes, that's it. They said time was important. They're waiting on the phone."

Jason's parents hurried into the house.

Susan's mum began gathering up the glasses and a plate of cookies from the table. "Susan, can you bring the jug, please?" she asked as she headed toward the front door.

"I'll bring the cushions," Susan's dad offered. He looked up at the sky. "It could rain."

By the time the things from outside had been stowed and Susan and her parents climbed the stairs to hear what had happened, Aunt Laura and Uncle John were sitting on either side of Jason on the couch.

Jason looked up and smiled at Susan as she drew near. "We're going home to Australia," he announced.

Aunt Laura explained, "I'd applied to have him included in an experimental program. There's a plant that they've heard about. It grows in the bush, and there are signs that it may be able to reduce cancer cells significantly."

"I am so hopeful for you." Susan's dad sank into an armchair. "When will you have to leave?"

Uncle John spoke up. "As soon as we can get a flight."

Susan's mum slapped her hands on her thighs. "Then let's get all the clothes that need washing in the machine."

Aunt Laura stood. "Good idea. Thanks, Alice." The two hurried off, all business.

Uncle John stood, too. "Stewart, can we go to your office to make some phone calls?"

"Of course."

Susan plopped down on the couch. "I am going to miss you so much." She reached over and ruffled Jason's hair. "My next adventure won't be the same without you along." Susan thought about it for a moment. "You made it all better for me."

Jason nodded. "Maybe if this cure works, we can have other adventures together. I'd like that."

Susan patted his knee. She didn't speak—her heart was too full. She held Jason's hand in the pool of quiet that gathered around them.

Presently Susan stood. "Wait here," she ordered and left the room.

She ran out to her mother's studio and over to her workbench. She couldn't decide between the crystals she had grown and the stones she had carved into smooth, pleasing shapes. *A stone, I think.* She fondled them until she found her best one. *This one.*

She held it in her hand. She had carved a piece of pale green soapstone. It fitted snugly into the palm of her hand. The edges were smooth, but she had worked a deep groove across the center of the stone. At one edge she had gouged a little rough spot. She ran her thumb along the groove. Smooth. Her little finger curved down to poke at the rough area. Perfect. *This is the one.*

She hurried back to Jason. He was sitting quietly where she had left him.

She felt a little shy now that she was standing in front of him. She stooped down and started gathering up the jigsaw pieces. Jason stayed quiet and still.

As she lifted a handful of pieces onto the table, she saw that Jason was watching her. He looked sad and frail.

What could she say? "You know, it was you. You were the important one on our trip." She nodded, becoming more certain as she spoke. She sat next to him. "You saved the emperor. That's when the crystal decided it was time for us to leave." She pushed his shoulder gently. "You coming with me wasn't an accident. You were meant to be there to save Frederick."

Jason smiled. "Yeah, I did, didn't I?"

"Look." Susan pulled out the carved stone. "I made this. I want you to have it."

Jason took it carefully from her hand. "It's beautiful," he said. "Thank you." Jason ran his thumb along the groove. "It feels good." He leaned over and gave her a kiss on the cheek.

"Erm," Susan rubbed her cheek in surprise. "Let's Google Frederick and see if he turned out to be a good Emperor."

Jason nodded. "Good idea. Help me up."

Susan pulled him to his feet and put his arm around her shoulder to help him across the room to the desk where her computer sat.

AUTHOR'S NOTE

In the year 1212, history tells us that thousands of children took to the roads of Europe, all travelling to free the Holy Land. Susan and Jason interact with children travelling through the lands of the Holy Roman Empire.

People like Grefin travelled through the countryside and gathered groups together to meet Nicholas, their leader, in Cologne. From there they travelled along the Rhine and over the Alps to the city of Genoa. Many, many died along the way, particularly in crossing the Alps, which is a range of very high mountains.

Tragically, the few who reached Genoa, found that the sea did not part for them as Nicholas had promised. The city of Genoa offered to take in any who wished to stay, and many did, but some straggled back into Germany.

At the same time, in France, a shepherd boy, had a vision that he should lead the children to the king to insist that the king lead another pilgrimage to the Holy Land. They marched across France. The king wouldn't hear them so they marched to the Mediterranean. Many were offered passage on ships only to find themselves sold as slaves.

History calls these two events the Children's Crusades. I have not used the word crusade in Lady Knight, as it was a word brought into use when the knights going to the Holy Land began to wear a large red cross on their tunics. In the time of our story the children were considered pilgrims.

Frederick II did become Emperor of the Holy Roman Empire. He was 19 years of age when he was crowned. His Grandmother was called Beatrice, but I don't know if he had a cousin called Katerina.

There was an assassination attempt when he travelled to meet the French Prince. No-one knows how he knew in advance that it would occur.

The city of Lake Constanz stood for him in the face of Otto IV's army, so it seemed reasonable to assume that he had entered the city earlier, to form alliances.

King John of England, really was the uncle of Otto IV. Otto grew up in the English Court, and King John supported his right to be Emperor.

The Hohenstaufen vs Welf rivalry was very true and persisted for generations.

If you want to learn more about this period in history there are many books and stories available. It was a turbulent time. I hope my book Lady Knight has given you a sense of what it was like to live and travel in the year 1212.

ACKNOWLEDGEMENTS

I wish to say thank you to many people. There is so much to be done to take a story from my head to a book and then to have that book placed in the hands of readers.

Lock has spearheaded the marketing efforts. He has ensured that my name and my books are out there in places where the public can find them. He produced the videos that are playing on YouTube, Facebook, www.grosemaryludlow.com and beyond.

Jin Wang, held our hands through the creation of a web-site I feel very proud of. Diogo Lando produced another striking cover for us. Haleigh, my Create Space editor pulled it all together for me and offered helpful insights that made my story better.

My writer friends, Roberta Rich and Irene Watts are there for me every inch of the way. Their helpful insights have led me on. Thank you.

This is the tip of the ice-berg as far as acknowledgements go, but I hope you all know how much I appreciate your help, encouragement, and input.

BIOGRAPHY
G. ROSEMARY LUDLOW

G. Rosemary Ludlow is a former schoolteacher with a deep love for storytelling and teaching children to read. She is honored and grateful that her first book in the *Crystal Journals* series, *A Rare Gift*, was shortlisted for the Chocolate Lily Awards. When she isn't thinking up new and exciting stories, she enjoys spending time with family and friends, reading, flying in helicopters, sailing in boats, and taking lots of pictures.

G. Rosemary Ludlow is a storyteller.

Visit my Web site: http://grosemaryludlow.com/
Subscribe for all the latest news.

Email me: g.rosemary@comwave.com

CPSIA information can be obtained
at www.ICGtesting.com
Printed in the USA
FSOW04n1543300917
39180FS